Rose in Bloom

by
E.J. Swanson

authorHOUSE

AuthorHouse™
1663 Liberty Drive, Suite 200
Bloomington, IN 47403
www.authorhouse.com
Phone: 1-800-839-8640

© 2008 E.J. Swanson. All rights reserved.

No part of this book may be reproduced, stored in a retrieval system, or transmitted by any means without the written permission of the author.

First published by AuthorHouse 10/16/2008

ISBN: 978-1-4389-0964-6 (sc)

Printed in the United States of America
Bloomington, Indiana

This book is printed on acid-free paper.

Table of Contents

Unremarkable Beginning	1
Shy Girl	3
Lunch Date	13
Dinner for Two	24
Turning Point	38
Newfound Freedom	45
Back to School	52
A Chance Encounter	61
Free at Last	69
Decision	74
Relaxing at last	77
Pursuit	81
Return to the Library	87
Unexpected Visit	94
Afternoon Interlude	97
Try and Try Again	102
The Poacher	105
Help Wanted	113
Found at Last	116
Getting Intimate	125
Untamed Woman	134
Whisked Away	138
Grecian Sun	146

Realization	169
Alone Again	180
Naked Strangers	184
Game On!	193
And Then There Were Two	212

Unremarkable Beginning

If there was one thing you could say about Samantha Sinclair it was that she was unremarkable. She lived in an unremarkable town, on an unremarkable street. She worked in what was to her mind probably the most unremarkable of jobs, a librarian in that unremarkable town.

Her mousey-brown hair was always tied back in a neat little bun. Although she usually wore lipstick it was always shades that were so subtle as to be almost invisible. The black horn-rimmed glasses she sported were mostly for show as the prescription was so weak she rarely really needed them. She mostly liked them for the visual effect it gave her when she looked down over them at the library patrons. She imagined herself as a stern authority figure, commanding those around her, but really the patrons saw her as an unremarkable librarian, trying to appear more important than she really was.

Bland grays and tans were her usual fare in wardrobe, occasionally with a black belt and shoes (the extent to which she would "let herself go wild"). Once she had even permitted herself to put on a flashy gold chain her father had given her when she was a teenager, but she guiltily hid it beneath her turtleneck sweater.

She had friends at the library with whom she occasionally would share an unremarkable lunch of soup and a sandwich. After work though she declined all invitations to go out with them. She preferred to spend quiet evenings at home with her cat Dilly, an unremarkable mottled orange tabby that she had adopted some years back. Or had he adopted her? She was never quite clear on that.

Once in a very long while she would date an unremarkable man, who would take her to an unremarkable restaurant or movie. If he were especially polite she might allow him a quick peck on the cheek goodnight. She rarely allowed the same man to take her out twice though (and oddly enough the opportunity rarely came up anyway).

But destiny has an odd way of playing tricks with us. It sets us up in our nice comfortable niches, and then opens the floor up beneath us, sending us to hitherto unknown fates.

If there was one thing you could say about the destiny of Samantha Sinclair, it's that it was decidedly **not** unremarkable.

Shy Girl

It was a quiet day in the library and Samantha tried to keep herself busy by searching through the stacks, ensuring everything was filed correctly. It was a tedious task at the best of times but it gave her a certain sense of peace and order. No interaction was required with the teenagers who would never set foot in the place unless their teacher ordered them too, or tried to surf for pornography on the library computers. She didn't have to explain yet again to ignorant first-timers that the Dewey Decimal System had nothing to do with ground moisture.

Samantha sighed to herself, and became lost in her thoughts as she methodically went through each aisle, each row, and each shelf. Her thoughts were interrupted briefly when she encountered a handsome young man searching studiously through the non-fiction section. She stood to one side, waiting for him to finish before continuing her work. The thought of striking up a conversation with him never occurred to her, and even if it had she would have been too embarrassed to do so. He was so good looking, why would he ever talk to someone as plain as her?

Finally he seemed to have settled on something and moved on to one of the nearby tables to pore over his find. Samantha continued her work, looking at the section he had just been in and tried to guess what he had selected based on what was still remaining. It was a little game she liked to play to keep her mind sharp. She had become quite good at it over the years.

Let's see, she thought to herself, what have we here. Scanning through the shelves Samantha found, to her surprise, the poetry of Keats, Byron, Shelley... Not at all what she would have expected a man like that to be looking through. Careful Samantha, she said to herself. "You're getting cynical now. Men have interests other than sports and naked women you know. Still she couldn't help but wonder if he had in fact picked up some misfiled baseball trivia book, or thought that Shelley was in fact Mary Shelley, author of *Frankenstein*.

Now cut that out, she chastised herself. He's probably a very sensitive man who has an appreciation for poetry. The little voice in the back of her head piped in with, Yeah and I bet his boyfriend likes it too. Samantha slammed the book she was looking at onto the shelf with a loud thump, mildly annoyed that she couldn't control her own inner voice. People looked up from their books in her direction. A fine example she was setting – the noisy librarian.

That decided it. She couldn't continue her work with this distraction inside her head. She had to find out the truth – just what was it that he had been looking for amongst all of this poetry? Glancing quickly over at him

Rose in Bloom

Samantha saw that though he had briefly looked up at the noise like everyone else he was now deeply engrossed in his selection.

Seeing him there Samantha let her thoughts wander. She imagined herself marching right up to him and striking up a casual conversation, then subtly turning the topic to his book in order to find out what he had chosen and why. Yeah right Samantha, she thought to herself. And while you're dreaming I'd like a new car and a cottage on the Rhine.

She shook off her daydream and, realizing she was not going to be able to continue with her task, headed back towards her desk at the front. No doubt somebody was waiting to ask her why they called them "stacks" when they were shelved sideways, or some other equally inane question. So lost in thought she was that she didn't notice her mystery man gazing at her. Oh my goodness, she thought. I bet I've been talking to myself and now he's wondering what kind of lunatic I am.

His eyes seemed steady, not wavering. Looking at her with what looked more like curiosity than incredulity; and something deeper. Something Samantha would have articulated as being 'behind his eyes', though the very thought seemed silly. He raised one finger and motioned her to come towards him. Samantha felt her breath catch. Did he want to see her? Now she was in trouble. No doubt he wanted to chastise her for distracting him from the very book with which she had been preoccupied. She glanced behind herself, to check if he wasn't motioning to someone else - his wife perhaps. Ever the optimist, aren't we? Samantha sniped to herself.

She was just about to mentally upbraid herself again for that thought when he repeated his gesture. Well there was no sense in delaying – might as well face the music. She gingerly walked over to the table he occupied. At least, she thought, I'll be able to see what that book is and get back to my work in peace.

Clearing her throat she said in her best librarian's whisper, "Is there something I can help you with sir?" Her eyes furtively glanced downwards hoping to catch a glimpse of the book's title but he was leaning forward on it, covering any identifying information. "Why yes miss, there certainly is." He had a very pleasing voice. Although he was keeping it quiet as well there was a hint of power behind it, as though he could fill the room with it had he the desire.

"I couldn't help but notice you were looking in the shelves for something, and I thought it might be the book that I've just picked up." Samantha relaxed somewhat. Not only was she not in trouble, but also he was going to voluntarily provide the information she had been seeking. She suddenly felt a little embarrassed as she realized that he didn't know she worked at the library so this was purely a social conversation.

Best to play it cool, she thought. Maybe that way I can actually talk with him without fainting. Indeed it had been a long time since she had carried on any sort of non-work related conversation with a man. Samantha had lost track of the time that had passed since she had parted ways with her previous boyfriend, although the term 'boyfriend' was probably too generous to the last man she had deigned to date more than once.

"Why no, actually. I was just checking the books to see that everything was filed properly." Very cool, Samantha congratulated herself with. Now keep breathing and you'll be fine.

"Oh, I see," he said. That should have been the end of the conversation but he didn't seem inclined to stop at this point. "Is everything in order then? I'd hate to think I had created a mess there." Samantha silently wished she could slink away from this conversation. She found it increasingly more difficult to continue coherently with that handsome smile facing her. "Y-ye-yes. Yes it is, thanks for asking."

"Smooth Samantha, smooth," she said, mentally kicking herself, but he seemed nonplussed and continued on. "That's good. I hate it when some thoughtless clod keeps comes through filing books willy-nilly. It really would be impossible to find anything if people were left to their own devices, don't you agree?"

Something in this man's friendly manner put Samantha at ease. Without thinking she replied, "I most certainly do. And don't you know that the very people who had caused the confusion in the first place would be at the front of the line to complain that they couldn't find what they wanted?"

Wow, she thought. Where did that come from? It certainly wasn't like her to speak to strangers, and giving a strong opinion like this was something she usually reserved for the privacy of her home and the friendly ears of her cat Dilly. The man seemed not to react to this sudden change of character in her, for indeed he knew nothing of her character and this might have been a perfectly normal reaction for her.

"My name is Dave," he said. "And I'm guessing that you work here, right?" Samantha was momentarily flustered, "That's right, how did you know?" "Simple deductive reasoning," answered Dave. "Not to mention the name tag on your shirt," he added with a chuckle.

"Oh my goodness how silly of me," Samantha blurted out. "I always forget I have this on. I'm so sorry about that. Well I guess you know my name too since that's on the badge as well. Silly little things they make us wear, as though anyone is going to address a librarian by name. The best I get is 'Miss', or 'You', or on particularly awful days 'Madam'. You'd think they'd at least let us retain our dignity and allow us to introduce ourselves instead of wearing a banner blurting our names out to the world."

Samantha froze and put her hand to her mouth. She had suddenly become aware of the inane schoolgirl babble that had been flying out of her. Her eyes widened as she examined Dave for any sign that he would run off looking for the men in the white coats to haul her away.

Thankfully she didn't see that. Instead what she saw was a man paying close attention to everything she was saying, as though it were the wisest musings of a guru. At long last he spoke. "I know exactly what you mean. The unofficial reason for nametags is to let people call you by your name so that you'll be inclined to ask for theirs and make them feel more comfortable. In practice though the only ones who use your name are the ones who would ask for it anyway so why bother putting a billboard on yourself?"

"Wow, he's intelligent too," thought Samantha. "I wonder if... nooo... There's no way someone like him would be even remotely interested in me." Dave picked up his book to show to her. In the flustered conversation Samantha had entirely forgotten that it was the reason she had ventured over here in the first place. "This is the book I was looking through," he remarked. "Filed correctly and everything."

"Th-tha-thanks," Samantha stammered, wondering to herself how he could have known that she was trying to sneak a peek of that book. "You have an interest in poetry then?" she continued, wondering further exactly what it was that kept words coming out of her mouth when all she really wanted to do was slink away and resume checking the books.

"Absolutely – ever since high school in fact. I managed to make it through English classes without having my love of the work be sabotaged by the boring analysis we always had to do." Dave seemed perfectly comfortable talking about poetry in this way – a manner in which Samantha knew from listening to others talk would be immediately frowned upon and call his manhood into question. Another thought floated through her head, but it was quickly interrupted…

"Would you like to get some coffee on your break? I'd love to share some of the things I've found with someone, and you seem like you'd be interested," offered Dave.

Samantha hesitated… It had been so long since she had been asked anywhere to do anything with a man that she barely recognized it as an offer. It seemed harmless enough, but she knew nothing at all of this man. "Well I do have somewhat of an interest in poetry," she said, stalling for time to think. "I'm not really much of a coffee person though."

Dave quickly jumped in, "No problem – the place I'm thinking of has a wonderful selection of teas, herbal teas, and probably the finest hot chocolate to be found north of the equator. Surely you've been to 'Human Beans', it's just across the street after all."

In truth Samantha had never set foot in the place, preferring to go straight home after work and never really taking a lunch break away from her own little desk. She didn't want to reveal this to Dave for some reason so it left her little choice but to blurt out, "Of course, hot chocolate does sound good on a chilly day like this."

"Okay then it's a date, I'll meet you there at noon," Dave confirmed. "A date??!?" thought Samantha. "Me on a date with this attractive hunk of man?" A little hard to believe for her but she managed to blurt out "Okay, see you then" before a young girl came up behind her and asked her where she could find "info about ancient Peruvian dudes or something". She smiled her polite librarian smile and took her off to the appropriate section.

"Peruvian dudes," she chuckled to herself. "I wonder what they would think of being called that." After doling out a brief lecture on the lifestyle and beliefs of the ancient Peruvians Samantha departed quickly and headed back to where she had left off sorting the shelves. To her disappointment Dave had left his spot at the table.

Turning to the shelves she resumed checking that everything was neatly in order. As usual she was finding books shuffled to the end of the shelf after being drawn out from the middle, the occasional upside-down book, and even one that was sitting there with the binding pointed in. "What on earth are these people thinking?"

she wondered, and pulled the book out to find its proper place. To her great surprise it was the book of poetry that Dave had been reading. She couldn't believe it – was his comment on books being misfiled just a line he was giving her? Was he some despicable gigolo toying with her?

She was so angry she was about to slam the book back into place and forget about her coffee "date" when she noticed something sticking out of the book. "Oh wonderful," she thought. "Not only has he turned it completely backwards, he's also torn a page." Carefully opening it so as not to cause further damage she was surprised by what she saw.

Inside the book the page was not torn at all, it was simply raised up to mark a location, and in a skillful manner that didn't damage the book at all. There was also a little slip of paper there, one of the standard ones scattered around the library to help people write down the reference information they needed (and to prevent them from writing same into the books).

Samantha picked up the piece of paper, curious as to its contents now. All it said was "13-19 – Dave". Clearly this was some sort of message left by Dave that she was intended to find. 13-19… it probably referred to the line numbers within the page that was marked. The left page ended at line 12 so clearly it had to be the right side. Samantha began reading the passage.

> *'Twixt the dust and ashes the flower settles in.*
> *Longing for the first breath of spring,*
> *Longing for a better place in the world.*

This was very interesting indeed! It seemed Dave was somewhat of a romantic. Samantha eagerly read the remainder of the poem

> *The sunshine beams upon it, the flower cannot tell.*
> *That within those silvery beams lay its salvation.*
> *At long last the petals do unfold,*
> *Beauty everlasting and a wonder to behold.*

The style's a bit odd, thought Samantha, but what a wonderful thought. She wondered why Dave had marked this particular passage for her to look at. At length she decided that the best way to find out would be to meet him at the appointed hour and ask him herself. So, she mused. A man of mystery as well as a romantic. Dangerous combination.

Lunch Date

The remaining hour before lunch fairly flew by as Samantha continued on her self-appointed errand of arranging all of the shelves. She had just moved onto the reference area when she suddenly noticed the time – 12:05, she was late! Rushing back to her desk she quickly put up her 'out to lunch' sign and donned her jacket. Knowing it was a little chilly out she debated with herself, I know it's just across the street but that cool air always has such an effect on my…ummm… modesty that I really do need the jacket.

Her co-workers were surprised to see her dashing out the front door so quickly. Ordinarily she wandered out at a leisurely pace, and only on those rare occasions she didn't stay in the library and eat at her desk. "No doubt I've set several tongues wagging," she chuckled to herself. "Honestly, you'd think they'd never seen someone leave for a date before."

That thought froze Samantha in her tracks. She was indeed going on a date. Scarcely believing her own audacity in talking to this stranger in the first place she was now heading out to meet him in public! Maybe it wasn't such a good idea after all. Maybe she should just stay in, and he would go away, possibly disappointed but at least her own life would stay neat and tidy, as it had always been. She remembered her mother's words "A woman works her whole life to arrange her life in a careful manner and then looks for some man to knock everything flying." Was that really what she wanted?

Oh come on Samantha, for goodness sakes it's just a coffee. It's not like you're incredibly attracted to the man and want him to drag you off like some wild aboriginal and make mad passionate love to…. you… oh dear. Samantha stood at the front door, realizing what her thoughts implied and even more uncertain of what to do. On the one hand she did want to know what the passage in the poem meant, but on the other… well she couldn't really come up with a good other hand but she knew there must be one somewhere and that it was the source of her nervousness.

"Samantha, over here!" called Dave, who had spied her from inside the coffee shop. "Oh well," sighed Samantha, "I guess I have no choice but to go now, as awful as it might be." She strode inside and tried to give no hint of the trepidation she was feeling. It was entirely unnecessary of course since it was a particular talent of hers to keep her emotions under tight control so that nobody really had a hint of what she was feeling. "Hello Dave, nice to see you again", she said pertly.

Determined as she was not to raise the subject herself it just seemed to flow out of her – "So what exactly did that passage of poetry mean?" Dave laughed and smiled. Such a nice smile it was too… big broad cheeks expanding, teeth warmly exposed, his eyes lighting up along with the rest of his face. "I would have thought that was obvious," he said, but went no further.

"No, it was not obvious and I'd appreciate your not laughing at me thank you very much," Samantha snapped, more embarrassed than angry at Dave's reaction. That bright smile of his emerged once more as he patiently replied, "That's okay, I bet you knew what it was and just aren't ready to see it yet. That passage was about you Samantha."

Samantha's thoughts flashed back to the exact wording once again when realization dawned on her. "So I'm supposed to be the flower, the library is the ash in which I dwell? I guess that makes you the sunbeam come to free me then does it?"

Dave was suitably impressed. With just that small hint Samantha picked up on the entire meaning in a matter of seconds. "Precisely," he replied. "That is, if you want to be freed."

"Such impertinence," Samantha said aloud. Normally she would just think such things to herself but for some reason this could not be held inside. "I can assure you that I am not in any kind of prison or danger from which I need your extrication help. I am not some damsel in distress for you to come charging in on your white horse and snatch me from the jaws of this supposed dragon. And even if I were, what on earth makes you think that you are capable of doing such a thing?"

Samantha glanced around the coffee shop, noticing the other patrons looking up from their newspapers and cell phones at her tirade. She was not embarrassed this time. In fact, she felt oddly light and free for having said this.

Dave however was like the proverbial rock, standing fast while Samantha's words washed over him, seeming to have no effect whatsoever. Instead, he leaned over towards her and whispered conspiratorially into her ear, "What you just said confirms what I've suspected. You have a great confidence inside you, but have refused to let it out. I would be willing to bet that you've never made love; fearing that the smoldering woman inside of you would be too much for you to handle."

A great indignation was rising within Samantha. In fact she greatly desired to be very angry with this man but so far he had told her nothing but the truth, and been nothing but pleasant and gentle in doing so. Still this comment required a response so she whispered back to him, "My love life, sir, is none of your business, and I can handle myself quite well thank you."

Though hardly believing that would be the end of it what Dave said next caught her dumbfounded. "Well then prove it. You've wanted to make love to me since the moment you laid eyes on me in the library. But even meeting me here for coffee was a great effort for you, and now you are hiding your desires behind this phony indignation that others may buy, but I can see right through."

Not quite sure how to answer this Samantha sat for long seconds, mouth agape as her thoughts raced through the events of the past few hours. Why **had** she come here to meet him, going against every facet of her normal routine? Why had she not walked out on him when he immediately became so personal and intimate? Most importantly, why could she not think of a single shred of evidence to contradict him? There was no use denying it – she did indeed have a great desire to surrender herself to him. Maybe she should take a chance and express it.

"I have to admit," she ventured, "that the thought of being with you is arousing, as well as a bit frightening. After all, I hardly know you and I've always believed that love-making should be the end of intimacy, not the beginning."

Not showing any reaction to Samantha's shocking, at least to her, admission Dave replied, "Did you hear what you just said? '…the **end** of intimacy.' When two people share that experience it allows them to explore parts of each other they normally do not get to see. I think you have it backwards; it truly is the beginning of real intimacy."

Samantha was not sure what to think at this point. She was slowly realizing that her beliefs might just have been yet another way she used to keep men out of her life, and out of her bedroom. Was this man showing her the way to a deeper level of emotions, or was he just playing on her fears in order to add a notch to his bedpost?

Dave said nothing while she sat there thinking, idly stirring her now-cold cup of mochaccino. Samantha's thoughts drifted to begin wondering what he would look like lying back against her oak headboard, clad only in that radiant smile. She imagined what it would feel like to have his skin pressed against hers in a feverish pitch shared long into a lazy afternoon.

At length she came to a decision. "Okay Dave; let's say for the sake of argument that you have convinced me. What now?" Although the phrase itself seemed full of confidence and almost defiance Samantha felt anything but. In fact she was terrified of what he might have to say. "Maybe," that voice in the back of her head whispered, "Maybe he's right. Maybe you are afraid of real intimacy and avoid it at all costs."

Seemingly oblivious to Samantha's inner dialogue, Dave quickly answered, "Why then you come back to my place of course. I think you realize that we've already made a connection – an intimacy of sorts itself. It's only natural that we get together to further explore that connection; feel the boundaries of it through more personal contact, and try to further understand how our lives are touching each other."

That was the sort of answer Samantha was expecting, but it was phrased in such an odd but eloquent way that she had a hard time rejecting this obvious proposition out of hand. In fact she was seriously considering it when she felt the tips of Dave's fingers stroke her thigh. A warm tingle came over her entire leg and she looked up into his eyes.

"Now," he said, "If that small touch of mine meant absolutely nothing to you, or repulsed you then we can part now in peace with no regrets. If, however, it stirred something deep inside you – something so deep that you can't even tell where it's coming from yourself, then I think you know what you should do."

Samantha had to admit that there was something to what he was saying. The stirring he mentioned was undeniable and went far deeper than the mere surface reaction of her skin to his soft touch. Something inside her wanted him in a deep, dark, and positively primal way and was making its voice well known to her.

Rose in Bloom

Continuing to meet his gaze Samantha said slowly and steadily, "Dave – I want you to come back to my apartment and make love to me tonight." Samantha's quaking hands were suddenly steady. The expected catch in her throat never materialized. The deep flush she anticipated engulfing her face in a sea of crimson never rose. Despite the seeming incredulity of her words her body betrayed her – she had meant every word of it. In fact her body was already anticipating the pleasure to come. She felt a small drop of warm moisture run down between her thighs.

Unexpectedly Dave arose from the table, dropping a five-dollar bill on it for their coffee. Without answering or reacting he motioned for Samantha to follow him outside, which she did. Was this some kind of weird rejection? Did he want to take her outside so that she wouldn't make a scene? Why was she so willing to follow this man around without explanation or reason?

He seemed to increase his stride, staying a full pace ahead of Samantha as they exited the coffee shop and headed away from the library. Samantha briefly glanced at her watch to see that her lunch was almost over and became suddenly aware that she hadn't actually eaten anything. Looking back up she saw Dave turn the corner down the nearby alley and almost lost him. "Dave, where did you go?" she ventured.

"I'm over here," he replied. "To the left, beside the doorway." It was hard to see him where he stood but Samantha could easily tell where he was from the sound of his voice. She quickly skipped over to join him and playfully added, "Gotcha!" He jumped back slightly, not expected this kind of energy from Samantha so soon.

Smiling broadly he took her arm and pulled her towards him. "Yes, you got me alright. Now what are you going to do with me?"

Their lips were mere millimeters apart now. Samantha's heart was fluttering and she felt a little dizzy. Breathlessly she answered him. "I… I… think that I have you right where I want you now. I-It's not up to you to question my motives." With a sudden resolve Samantha closed the gap between them and placed her lips firmly onto Dave's. It had been a long time since she felt a man's touch in this way, but it was so natural.

Their hands explored each other as their kiss became more intense. Samantha's lips seemed to explode with pleasure as her and Dave merged into one, spinning and swirling together. She was vaguely aware of his hands running down her back and slipping inside her skirt. His touch was warm against her exposed legs and his fingertips tickled as they explored beneath the lace edges of her panties.

"Dave, wait…" Samantha tried to say, but the pull of the pleasure she was experiencing was too strong. "Never mind… keep going. It feels so good." His hand found it's way inside her panties. Now she could feel his bare skin against her own, stroking her, barely touching yet somehow pressed tightly into her. She turned her head to the side and let his mouth explore the side of her neck. He nibbled her earlobe and the sensitive spot beneath them, then ran his tongue around the edge of her ear sending shivers down her spine.

As she quivered under his touch her legs tightened up, trapping Dave's hand between them. His fingers continued to stroke her, feeling the edge of her lips, inflaming her desire. Samantha's toes felt like they would burst into fire – she needed to feel this man closer than any man had been before.

Reaching down Samantha took Dave's hand into her own. Reaching her other hand around his neck she drew him to her and pressed her lips tightly on him once more. In one swift motion as she did this her lower hand pressed against his, driving his fingers inside her. She felt her world explode as she held him even tighter, guiding his hand in circles and ensuring it kept contact with her as she did.

Not even knowing herself at this point Samantha was lost in her passion. She whispered into Dave's ear, "I want you now. I want you here and now, inside me. You know what I'm asking don't you?" Dave had clearly been overwhelmed by Samantha's onslaught. It was all he could do to answer by silently nodding his head and giving her a tighter squeeze. Samantha released his hand long enough to lower his zipper, feeling his hard cock below waiting for her. Pushing his underwear aside she pulled it out and guided it in to where his fingers currently rested.

He was bigger and warmer than she expected. She knew that a man's penis would be bigger than her own fingers but she wasn't really prepared for the sense of fullness it gave her. Drawing herself against him Samantha closed her eyes to deepen the sensation, relying on Dave to duplicate the motion she had been doing with his hand moments ago. Their lips remained together, one second playfully nibbling each other, the next diving together with enthusiasm.

The moment of her orgasm was unmistakable. It began as a quivering in her thighs that slowly spread through her entire body. She felt herself squeezing tightly on Dave inside her as each thrust shook her from head to toe. He too was shaking and moaning softly into her ear. Although Samantha had never experienced one firsthand before she knew this was what a man's orgasm must be like. She grabbed his ass and squeezed it tightly as she and Dave both rode the last wave of their orgasms into a breathless shivering pair, collapsing against the wall of the alley.

When Samantha finally regained her breath she straightened up her skirt and panties. She also buttoned up her shirt that Dave must have at some point opened, unbeknownst to her. She looked at her breasts to see a small hickey mark forming on one and realized how consumed she had been by her passion to not even notice such a thing.

Dave had just finished doing up his pants when Samantha looked over at him. "Ummm… thanks. I guess I needed that a lot more than I realized." Dave's smile was still present, if a little weary. "To tell you the truth," he said, "I never realized you had such a fire in you. I saw something in there but I didn't suspect…" he trailed off.

"Don't tell me you were overwhelmed by little old me?" Samantha said playfully. "The shy retiring librarian shocked the experienced man of the world?" Dave responded reluctantly, "I'm afraid so. I'm almost afraid to ask you out for dinner tomorrow now."

Laughing at this sudden showing of timidity Samantha responded, "Well what if I promise not to bite?… much." Dave chuckled back at her and said, "Oh I wouldn't want to be responsible for repressing that fiery temptress I just saw a moment ago. I think I can take my chances just this once. Shall I pick you up after work then?"

"I think you can," Samantha replied. The tone in her voice had clearly strengthened; there was a confidence there she was not used to, but greatly enjoyed. "Just make sure you're ready to treat me nicely. I'm very delicate you know." Dave looked back at her slyly and replied, "Somehow I think that 'delicate' is not a word that describes you, but you can count on me to treat you very nicely."

With that he turned away and left. Samantha slowly ambled her way back to the library, already a few minutes late from "lunch".

Dinner for Two

"Samantha, where is your head at?" chided Trudy. "That's the third time you've stamped that one book!"

Samantha looked down at the overlaid layers of ink on the card and smiled, embarrassed. "I guess I am kind of distracted. I have a dinner date after work and I can't seem to stop thinking about it."

"Ohhh, a date now is it. Congratulations, it's been a long time coming!" Trudy teased. "I guess I can stop working on the old spinster shawl I was knitting for you."

"Come on, I haven't been that bad have I?" Samantha replied, knowing the answer even as the question left her lips. "Okay so I haven't been out a lot. But I have a sneaking suspicion that's about to change."

"No doubt, if that smile and glow you've been sporting all day mean what I think they mean." Trudy cocked her head to one side and gave an exaggerated wink.

Samantha anxiously eyed the clock as it painstakingly edged its way towards five o'clock. Normally she enjoyed her work so much that the time just flew by but today her head was in the clouds and nothing seemed to get done.

"Oh for gosh sakes will you go home already?" chided Trudy. "At least then you won't be bugging us with your mooning about."

"Are you sure?" Samantha replied. "I mean, I don't want to leave you guys holding the bag here or anything.

"Trust us," chimed in Jane, who happened to be passing by from the circulations department. "It will be less work for us if you leave early."

"Thanks guys, I really appreciate that," Samantha said, bounding out the door.

Trudy looked over to Jane and remarked, "Y'know, I don't think she even knew we were being sarcastic there. Oh well, at least we don't have to watch Miss Sillypants fawning over some mystery guy."

"Yeah, I'm jealous too," added Jane, seeing right through Trudy's feigned indifference.

Arriving home Samantha looked at the clock and knew she'd never have time to do everything she wanted. "Okay, just the essentials," she said to nobody in particular. "A quick shower, do something with this rat's nest of a hairdo, some basic makeup, a dress, some shoes…oh good god I'll never be ready in time."

Anyone watching Samantha would have been reminded of a Scooby-Doo chase scene. She dashed from bedroom to bathroom, back and forth at random intervals struggling to make herself look her best. Every now and then a little voice in the back of her head reminded her that he had been attracted to her when she was at work and probably looking quite frazzled, but she successfully ignored it in favor of her running about. It was calming in a way to keep in motion.

Just as she was fastening her last earring the doorbell rang. Samantha took a second to compose herself, and then walked slow and calm to the door. There stood Dave in a slightly rumpled but presentable suit, taken aback at the sight of her.

"Wow, that is… ummm… well I think… uhhhh…" he stammered.

"What's the matter? Cat got your tongue?" teased Samantha.

"More like my eyes. You look stunning."

Samantha blushed slightly, glad that her effort had been appreciated. "Why thank you kind sir, flattery will get you almost everywhere."

"Almost you say. I wonder what it would take to get the rest of the way?" Dave responded curiously.

"That's for me to know and you to try and try again until you find out. Now let's go. You're taking me to a very nice place and I don't want to be late."

Dave walked down to his car while Samantha locked up. He was marveling at the transformation that had happened in her. Was this the same woman who looked like she would die of fright when he talked to her only a day earlier? He held the door for Samantha who fairly bounced inside. This was shaping up to be a fine evening already.

The restaurant was dim and romantic, lit by soft glowing yellow bulbs and flickering candles. Samantha had always wanted to eat here but it sometimes it didn't seem right coming here alone. The waiter quickly and

Rose in Bloom

unobtrusively took their order and left them to each other.

Samantha chatted on and on about the library, her family, her childhood – pretty much anything she could think of. It felt so good to talk to a real live man after so long she found it hard to stop, even knowing that she was probably boring him to tears.

Far from boring him this woman fascinated Dave. She seemed so open and honest. After their brief encounter yesterday he half-expected her to be so embarrassed that she wouldn't say a word to him. He wasn't particularly surprised by this change since he had seen a glimmer of it hiding in her, but to see it emerge so quickly was remarkable. It was as though she had kept it in a secret hiding place, just waiting to bring it out and show somebody.

As Samantha talked she became aware of Dave's foot, first playfully stroking her ankle, then slowly working it's way up and down her calf. It scared her for a brief moment. She wasn't afraid of **him** by any means. It was more like she had walked halfway across a very high bridge then suddenly looked down and realized where she was. This was not like her at all. What had come over her to be in this situation?

Seeing the sudden change in her face Dave smiled at her and said softly "Ahhh, there's that shy little girl I saw yesterday. Don't worry so much, you're in good hands… your own."

Samantha pondered just what it was he meant by that comment as his little game of footsie continued. She was suddenly emboldened and slipped off her shoe to do the same to him when their food arrived.

Looking nervously up at the waiter she wondered if he had seen what they were doing, as though it were a mortal sin that would get them ejected from the restaurant. If he did notice he gave no sign, placing their plates in front of them and offering to refresh their drinks before he vanished back into the kitchen.

They continued their little game through dinner. Dave never seemed to notice the various comings and goings of the waiter. His attention seemed to be solely on Samantha, gazing into her eyes while softly caressing her legs. Samantha went from fear, to acceptance, to excitement at their little naughty game. Maybe it was the wine, or the emboldening effect of the dim lighting, but something prompted her to lean over and whisper conspiratorially to Dave, "If you keep that up I'm going to need a cold shower when I get back."

Dave leaned in a little closer, brushing against her cheek. She could feel his breathe in her ear as he replied, "I know better ways for you to handle it back at your place, if you wouldn't mind me showing you."

Samantha felt a glow rising to her cheeks. It was more of an excited blush than an embarrassed one but the effect was the same. Laughing softly Dave remarked, "Come now, there's nothing embarrassing about me speaking my mind is there? Nothing at all shocking at me whispering in your ear how much I would greatly desire to make love to you? Nothing in my unhidden passion that would bring that blush to your cheeks?"

Samantha reached across to Dave and playfully whacked him on the shoulder. "Stop that, you evil man you. Challenging my virtue like that, of all the nerve. Besides, I'm not embarrassed in the least. It must be the candles making me hot. It couldn't at all be the thought of your naked body lying on top of mine, or the image of our warm skin rubbing together underneath the cool cotton sheets, listening to the strains of soft music. Not even the anticipation of the strong feelings you'll bring about between my legs over and over again."

This time Samantha was blushing for real. Her mouth seemed beyond her control now, just spouting off whatever words happened to pop up in her head. Sure she meant it, but polite girls don't say the kind of thing out loud…do they?

Of course Dave just continued to smile, turning the topic to something a little more innocuous as they finished their dinner. The dessert Dave chose for both of them to share was sinfully delicious and no doubt she was going to pay for it later, but sharing a single sweet confection between them was worth it. They playfully fed each other, each proclaiming that their side of the dessert was the superior one.

The bill arrived and before Samantha could even raise a protest Dave had dropped a (rather large) stack of bills onto it and stood up to leave. She hadn't really intended for him to pay the whole thing, but something in the way he had not even hesitated to handle it made her realize that he wouldn't allow her to help with it. At least not this time, she thought to herself, mentally filing away the event and determined to take him somewhere equally nice in the future.

The thought stopped her for a moment. Here she was already planning another date when they hadn't even finished this one, which was essentially their first. She must really like this guy. Either that or the fact that she hadn't gone anywhere with anyone in so long was making him seem wonderful by comparison. In any event the thought of another date was appealing to her so she continued to think of possible locations on the drive back to her place.

It wasn't long before Dave's car pulled up in front of her door. This was the moment of truth, she realized, not forgetting their conversation early in the dinner. Dave chose that moment to speak first, "Y'know it's getting awfully late…"

Samantha felt her eyes bulge, anticipating what he was going to say next. After all of that flirting he couldn't possibly be dumping her now could he? Surely she wasn't that undesirable that he had lost interest that quickly? Maybe she was too aggressive for him. She certainly had said some things she hadn't meant to. Could she have scared him off? Once again her mouth started before her mind had finished the thought. "Oh it's not so late, why don't you come in for a nightcap?"

There was that knowing smile again. "I was hoping you'd ask me. I just wanted to give you a graceful way out if you changed your mind."

Thumping him on the shoulder again Samantha laughed in burst of freed tension. "You brat, teasing me like that. You'd better get inside that door quickly before I make you regret it and cause a scene right here in front of the neighbors."

Not being able to resist Dave shot back, "In the hallway and everything? Oooh, you kinky girl. But it's a bit uncomfortable out here. Why don't I take a rain check for next time and settle for the bed for now?" Then he shot off towards the door, narrowly avoiding Samantha's hand before she took off after him.

"I win, that means I get to be on top," Dave proclaimed.

"No fair, you cheated by taking a head start," Samantha replied. "I declare your victory null and void and that means I'm the winner and I get to be on top."

"Well if you carefully read your racing manual, you'll notice it's clearly marked that whoever calls the start is allowed to leave immediately, even if their opponent was too lost in erotic daydreaming to notice that the race was on."

"Why you little…" began Samantha. "Lost in erotic daydreaming? Okay so maybe I was trying to remember what you look like naked, at least the parts I've seen, but I'd hardly call that daydreaming. More like…anticipation."

"Far be it from me to argue with a lady," said Dave as Samantha swung the door open for the two of them. "Tell you what; I'll declare a tie and we can both be on top."

"On top of what?" mocked Samantha.

"On top of that over there," replied Dave, pointing behind her. Not being entirely on her guard at that moment Samantha edged to the bedroom door to look at something that obviously didn't exist, affording Dave the opportunity to scoop her up into his arms. He took two large strides toward the bed and dropped her on it, slipped off his jacket, then jumping up immediately, pinned her down.

"I win again, high five!" Dave exclaimed. Samantha replied by reaching up to where he triumphantly kneeled atop her and flipping his shirt up over his head.

"Aha Mr. Champion, now you can endure the cold up there on your mighty peak."

"Speaking of peaks," Dave chuckled as he took hold of Samantha's blouse and pulled it straight off her, popping two of the buttons as he did so.

"You rat, that was one of my nicest blouses!"

Dave lowered himself down to Samantha's ear and breathed "I'll make it up to you". His mouth found her neck and he nibbled roughly on her, to which Samantha both giggled and shrieked. "Hey, not so rough you rotter."

"Oh-ho, I think I hear the tigress awakening. I knew there was one hiding in there somewhere."

"Tigress is it? Well tigress this buddy," Samantha shouted as she rolled and bucked, knocking him over, suddenly reversing their positions.

"So, the worm has turned now, so to speak. Gaze up at my magnificence now and be in awe!" Samantha couldn't believe how melodramatic she had suddenly become. She had never pictured herself capable of this kind of behavior at all, let alone in bed. It seemed entirely out of place and she felt a small amount of something. Was it guilt? Shame? Embarrassment? Whatever it was didn't seem to be mediating her behavior at all. It felt pretty good, somewhat liberating in fact.

Not entirely oblivious to her momentary lapse of attention Dave had been taking advantage of the situation, slowly lifting until he was in a position to reach around her. Samantha became suddenly aware of him and leaned forward to pin him back down.

"Thought you could get out that easily did you?" she chided.

A mischievous grin came over Dave's face. "Not at all," he replied. "I just wanted to be able to do this." With that he folded his arms over his head, taking Samantha's bra with him.

"Now the view is much more magnificent, and I am still in awe."

Samantha knew what she wanted then, and to her surprise she reacted immediately to get it.

"Oh but the view is much better... up close," she said as she dropped forward, her breast falling into his waiting mouth. Dave responded eagerly, almost savagely, rolling her nipple around in his mouth, using his tongue to explore the round surface of first one breast, then the other. For Samantha's part she was more than willing to passively accept this attention being heaped on her. Despite their previous encounter this felt like something she had not done in a very long time.

It could have been moments or hours that they lay there, exploring each other, hands sliding over their bodies as the stack of clothing next to the bed steadily grew. Soon it was just the warmth of their skin in close contact, as they left no inch of each other untouched.

Samantha had never felt so free before. It wasn't just the sex, which was without a doubt the best she had ever experienced. There was something else. Like part of her had been kept in a cage and had suddenly discovered that the door was never locked. She had only to open it and venture outside.

"Outside? No my dear, quite the opposite." Samantha blushed momentarily, realizing she must have been daydreaming out loud and he had heard the last little bit. Not wanting to admit he had once again caught her attention wandering Samantha quickly replied, "Your wish is my command," and slid down slowly, feeling him enter her inch by joyful inch.

The two of them spent hours in this playful manner. Once or twice Samantha had slipped into one of her daydreams but the sheer pleasure of the moment kept drawing her back out.

The end of the evening found them both laying together, entwined in each other's arms. The bed sheets lay scattered over the floor along with their clothing. The pillows had made valiant attempts to join them but kept being returned to their nest as one or the other of the couple needed a little extra support or softness.

Neither of them wanted to break the silence that surrounded them. Dave lay against Samantha's chest, listening only to the rapid beating of her heart while she felt his pressed against her waist, drumming in time with hers.

Finally it was Dave who spoke. "Samantha, I have to tell you that you took me totally by surprise there. I mean I knew that you weren't exactly the shy introverted librarian you seemed to be but...wow."

"Just a few short days ago if you had told me that someone would say that of me I would have thought you crazy. I **was** that shy introverted librarian until I met you. I don't know what you did or how you did it but I have to give you credit for this woman you've created."

"No Samantha, I haven't created anything. That woman was there all along. For one reason or another she thought she needed to hide and I just brought her out to play. I don't know why she was hiding but I sincerely hope that she'll be out more often."

Rose in Bloom

"Me too. Oddly enough I can't think of any reason why I had kept that bottled up inside me. All I know is that it feels amazing to let it out. I can see now everything I've been holding back being that shy librarian. I do believe I've even decided what I want to be when I grow up!"

Dave had to chuckle at that. "It's odd that you should phrase it that way. Something I read once convinced me that you should always be asking yourself that question, no matter what your age or experience. It's a way of keeping your dreams alive and refreshed. So tell me, what is it that you want to be? Astronaut? Ballerina? Lion tamer maybe?"

"Oh stop, I'm being serious," Samantha said, slightly disapproving, and punched him playfully in the arm.

"Ow, so am I. Well maybe not about that lion tamer thing, but the rest was dead serious."

"Okay, since you twisted my arm, and were **very** nice to my other parts," she winked, "I'll tell you. I've always wanted to study ancient history, and maybe some archaeology. Go on some digs and look at ruins. Do that whole 'Indiana Jones' thing."

"Really? Well I guess that explains the librarian part of you - gathering, sorting, and analyzing information. What makes ancient history so fascinating?"

"Oh I don't know. Maybe it's just the sense of wonder in looking back at great human achievements. At one time I had applied to get my degree but I just couldn't go through with it."

"Why not?" Dave was actually interested in this. In her boring little aspirations. The last boyfriend she had told about this just glazed his eyes and stared into space when she talked about here interests but Dave was keenly attentive. It felt good to have an audience, and more importantly a sympathetic ear.

"I don't know. Maybe I wasn't really suited for it to begin with. Maybe I didn't think I had the brains to get through it. Whatever the reason after I was accepted I just let the paperwork sit in a pile and never responded. I would imagine I'm on some secret blacklist somewhere, along with all of the other people who dared turn the school down."

"Well as an expert in the field of human psychology," Dave said, in a tone which obviously contradicted his statement, "It sounds to me like you are still a bit frightened about going there. In fact I'd be willing to bet that you won't do it."

Samantha was about to grudgingly agree with him when a little voice in the back of her head suddenly decided to make an appearance through her mouth. "Put your money where your mouth is mister because I'm going to do it. In fact I'm going to march right into the admissions office tomorrow and demand they take me. Then I'm going to go to the library and quit my job – it's sucked the life out of me for long enough."

Samantha's eyes bulged wide at the sound of her own voice making these outrageous claims. But then a firm smile came over her face along with the assurance that not only did she really mean it but it would really happen too.

Always quick to latch on to the opportunity Dave shot back, "Okay Ms. Big Shot, since you've accepted my bet without knowing the terms I get to set them."

The protest died in Samantha's throat before it even started. She was curious to hear what he had in mind.

"If I win this bet and you don't do these things," he continued, "Then you have to cook me dinner in the nude and do everything I ask of you while you are cooking. And believe me I plan to do a **lot** of asking."

"I guess I suckered myself into accepting that one, but what happens if I **do** go through with it?"

Dave hesitated slightly. Something in her tone told him right then that he had already lost the bet, but his honor wouldn't let him leave it uneven. "The same deal of course. I'm a decent enough cook, and I'll trust your imagination to be tame enough for me to handle. In fact I'll be overly generous and give you a whole week, even though you said you would do it all tomorrow."

"That's two things you're wrong about," smirked Samantha. The adrenaline rush from her bold pronouncement was still running through her. She seized the opportunity to pounce on him once more. "You're well-rested enough to argue with me, so you won't mind if we resume our interrupted love-making session I trust?"

In fact the effects of her earlier energy had exhausted Dave but her enthusiasm snapped him out of it and he was looking forward to having those luscious legs around him once again.

Turning Point

Two days later Dave received a phone message from Samantha consisting only of the words, "Marciano's - Noon". Surely Samantha wouldn't be giving in so early. It would be disappointing if she didn't at least give it a try until the end of the week.

Dutifully he showed up at the restaurant at the appointed time to find Samantha already there, waiting for him. As he approached the table she stood up and threw her arms around him. "There you are my big cuddly bear."

Briefly Dave wondered how many glasses of wine she'd gone through while waiting for him. A glance at the wall clock showed that he was exactly on time so it wasn't like she had to pass the time waiting for him.

Samantha must have noticed the quizzical look on his face. Answering his unasked question she continued, "No David I am not drunk. At least not on anything but life and my newfound freedom."

Suddenly Dave knew exactly what Samantha was drunk on. "You didn't…did you?"

"You bet your britches I did, and don't think my gratitude is going to spare you from coming through on that bet. It was a good thing you gave me extra time too since I failed to notice that I claimed I would do everything on a Sunday when nobody with authority is in the library and the school registration office is closed. Fortunately your overconfidence proved your undoing. I went in first thing this morning and signed up for a mature student course for a degree in Ancient History, then I went and quit my library job."

"Samantha you nut, how are you going to pay for the course if you don't have a job?" Dave was hoping a little dose of reality might calm her down a bit and at least get them safely back to their table.

But Samantha was having nothing to do with her calm cool logical side today. "I have no idea. All I know is that I couldn't continue there. It would have killed my dream, just when I finally managed to revive it again. Of course I had to enroll first before quitting, just on the off chance they refused me. No sense being too stupid about it," she chuckled, although Dave could tell she would have quit the job either way for exactly the reason she had just stated.

"Well I'm proud of you. That's an amazing step to take, and I know you'll be great."

Something about the way he said it led Samantha to believe there was something at the end of that sentence that was left out. The old Samantha would have just ignored it and continued on with her side of the conversation, or left the empty silence. The new Samantha had to know. "I hear a 'but' at the end of that sentence. What's up?"

"You're right, there is a 'but' there," Dave admitted, being ever more impressed at Samantha's sudden emergence from her cocoon. "'But' as much as I'd love to be around to share it with you and see you achieve your dreams like I know you will, my company just transferred me to Canada. I'm gone for a minimum two years, and they want me to leave at the end of the month."

There was a long pause as Samantha gathered her thoughts. After this huge transformation he had brought out in her he was going to leave? Was he just using her for some unknown purpose? Did he not care for her at all? Was there something wrong with her that drove him away?

In truth it was none of those. The sadness in Dave's eyes soon gave away the awful reality of the situation to Samantha. A thousand different possibilities flashed through her mind but in the end she knew that to stay with Dave one of them would have to give up on their dream, and that she could never allow. Not any more. She managed to pull up a brave smile onto her face and turned to him.

"Dave, I can never repay what you've done for me. I know you're thinking that I just did it myself but I couldn't have done anything without you. I also know that there's no way that we can stay together right now, but I'm willing to let the future happen the way it's meant to. I'm going to really miss you when you're gone, but there's one thing I'd like you to do for me before you go."

"Of course Samantha, I'd do almost anything for you, and I'm glad you realize that."

A little life returned to Samantha's face as her smile first warmed up, then returned to her mischievous grin. "We can pack an awful lot of loving into two weeks if you're agreeable. Sure you'll be busy preparing and whatnot but I'm claiming all of the spare time you have for myself. After all, you'll have plenty of free time while you're freezing up in Canada and missing me to pieces."

Dave hadn't realized what a worried expression he must have worn until he felt it relax at just that moment. "Not only do I agree, I absolutely insist on it. If the next two weeks are anything like the other night they may have to pour me into an envelope and mail me there but I won't regret it for a moment."

"All right then, it's agreed. And we're starting tonight, where you'll repay that bet of yours. I'll be kind and not ask for bacon or any other sizzling greasy dish, but other than that I plan on being quite demanding."

"I wouldn't miss it for the world," Dave smiled. "Come over at 5:30. I'll be just home from work and will need a shower to get ready. I'll leave the door open and you can start your demands there."

...

The next two weeks were bliss for Samantha. She'd been released from the monotonous repetitive demands of the library for the first extended time in ages, and she had the time of her life every night, the entire weekend, and one memorable lunchtime. Although technically she was between jobs it was the best "vacation" she had ever had.

Dave's departure was bittersweet. Through the course of the past two weeks Samantha had begun to blossom even further. Although she felt total affection and even love for him she began to realize that she would quickly grow beyond him. In a way it was better that he was leaving now, so that their parting came at a great time in their relationship.

Dave seemed to feel the same thing, although he expressed it in different ways. It was so easy to love this woman Samantha was turning into. She had become in many ways something he aspired to be. Her playful freedom was not locked down by any of the false social impediments that plagued so many people. She said what she felt, and didn't back down when she knew was right. Yet she readily admitted when she was wrong, and listened attentively. It was hard to see where these qualities had come from but it seemed that Samantha was destined to grow beyond anything he had to offer.

They embraced at the airport – the slow clutching embrace of people never to see each other again, not wanting to let go. One last kiss passed between them and he was off. Samantha cried to herself softly as she returned home. It was the right thing to happen, but that didn't make it any easier. Something beautiful had died, perhaps before its time, perhaps right on schedule. Nonetheless it was an occasion for mourning.

Normally Samantha would have found solace in her books. Feeling a slight weakness she gave in and returned. Not to the library though. That place was shut off from her until she felt she could handle all that it represented. The bookstore however didn't hold quite as much emotional power so she went there to peruse through its holdings.

Nothing much was catching her interest that night, so lost in her own thoughts was she. She wished that she had somebody close enough to her to confide in, to share

Rose in Bloom

her pain and commiserate with. Another side effect of the years in the library, she said to herself. I made lots of acquaintances and working buddies but no real friends whom I can count on when the chips are down.

Just then she looked up and found that she had wandered into the office supplies aisle. She was just about to leave and give up on this hopeless quest when something caught her eye. It was a journal. Not an accounting journal, but the kind that you write your thoughts in. A generation ago it would have been known as a diary, but that name was filled with associations to giggling young teenagers, not the serious thoughts of an adult.

On an impulse she picked it up and thumbed through it. Blank pages with nothing but the flourish at the top of the pages with the word "Thoughts" greeted her. For some reason opening the book soothed her somewhat. Out of the blue she realized she had been throwing the baby out with the bathwater. There was no sense in severing her connection with books, reading, and writing. These were things she loved, even if the social situation of a librarian managed to drive some more admirable traits of hers underground.

This journal promised to be just the thing she needed. She loved to write, and she needed a sympathetic ear to listen to her troubles, fears, hopes, and aspirations. Why not do both and keep a journal?

"I'll do it," she said out loud, waiting for the hushing noise that never came. The conditioning of the library didn't wear off so easily, but here was a friend she could pour that out to, who wouldn't judge her, would listen attentively, and would always be there when she needed it.

So sure was she that this was the right thing to do that she marched straight home and began writing in it immediately.

"First I'll properly identify you so that you don't get lost," she said to the journal. She neatly lettered her name on the inside cover.

"Now then," she continued, "If you're to be my confidante then we must be properly introduced." She opened up the journal to the first crisp blank page and began to do just that.

> *Dear Journal: Or should I say "Hello Journal". My name is Samantha Sinclair, but you can call me Sam. I think it suits me better now. I live at 154 Barclay Road, where you'll be living for now on as well. You can call me anytime at 905-555-7267. I'm always willing to listen to your problems as I hope you'll be willing to listen to mine. I guess I should start by telling you exactly how it came to pass that you became mine...*

Newfound Freedom

Well Journal, I finally did it. I finally landed myself a job to pay for my studies. About time too since the savings were just about gone. At least I had some time to ease myself back into schoolwork without the immediate pressure of a job.

You'll be happy to know that I decided not to pursue that career in modeling that I was telling you about. Mainly because the weight they wanted me to get down to was downright unhealthy, but don't think I wouldn't have done it! The girls there make good money and I'm proud of my ... ahem ... natural assets.

Sam looked at her latest journal entry and wondered what a real friend would have thought about that. She was telling the truth there and in cases like this where her decisions may have been socially questionable it was nice to have a non-judgmental ear on her side. A couple of girls in her classes seemed sympathetic but she didn't know them well enough yet to trust them with her innermost thoughts.

In fact there was a little white lie hiding in her truth there. She knew that if she had gone to work in a strip club the quality of man she would meet might not be up to the standards she was after. In fact since Dave left she hadn't even thought about men but it was getting to be time. She had released her sexuality and was eager to explore it more. The strip club would certainly have afforded her many opportunities to do so but she wanted a man who could make love to her mind and not just her body. Perhaps that was a holdover from her librarian days but in this case she felt it was a good thing to save.

In fact she had landed a job as a bartender at a local watering hole. The schedule was just flexible enough to let her get to her night classes yet still work enough hours to pay for school and the necessities. It only took her a week or so to learn the ropes. Her love of books had paid off, making it a breeze for her to remember and use all of the mixed drink recipes she was likely to run into. Mostly it was just uncapping and pouring beer anyway, this being a college town. Students couldn't afford much more, and barely that. Students like me, she often thought proudly to herself.

Most nights were fairly uneventful. The occasional rowdy drunk was the worst that Sam ever had to deal with. The fringe benefits were nice too. Since so many of the students hung out at this bar there was no shortage of eligible and good-looking young men. Plus she had the instant assurance that they were at least reasonably intelligent, being in college and all (although as she was to eventually learn this correlation was by no means perfect).

Despite all of the opportunities though none of these guys seemed able to even make a decent effort to ask her out. Maybe they thought she was too old (horrors!), maybe she was unapproachable (double horrors!), or maybe she was just so intelligent that she intimidated them (yeah, that's the one). Fortunately, or unfortunately – depending on your point of view, her newfound freedom would not let her be content with waiting for someone to come to her.

The evening was drawing to a close and Sam was just finishing up. Only one lone customer remained before she could shut down and he was nursing his drink. Sam sighed and supposed that she'd have to stick it out to the end with this one. At least he was cute. Usually the ones staying late are desperate for attention. After last call the place had cleared out pretty fast so it was only the two of them in the entire area now.

Sam decided to chat with him since it looked like they would be stuck together now anyway. She found him to be quite pleasant to talk with - witty and intelligent. Not at all what you'd expect from someone who had spent all night at the bar. It turned out that he was just out celebrating with friends and they had left early but he wanted to stay and enjoy the atmosphere a while longer.

In fact, with a little more chatting Sam found out that the "atmosphere" he was interested in was Sam. He became bolder as she showed interest, telling her what a nice body she had and how pleasant her personality was. Sam's thoughts began to drift, wondering if he had been undressing her with his eyes as they wandered up and down her curves. She playfully slapped him and ventured, "Hey you, quit staring at my breasts," and chuckled. He just smiled and replied, "Sorry, I'm sure you must get that all of the time with such a lovely figure." Sam blushed and confessed that she hadn't really, to which he continued, "Get out. You're putting me on. Why any man would be crazy not to be turned on by your mature sexy body."

Smiling again Sam said, "I'll take the word 'mature' as a compliment for now, and I must admit I've suspected men of watching me. Even the occasional woman," she added, "but none of them ever seems to do anything about it other than look." He looked into her eyes and boldly ventured, "That's their mistake then, and one I had better not make." With that he wrapped his arms around her and placed their lips firmly together. Squeezing her tight his tongue ran playfully over hers as Sam eagerly returned his kisses.

Sam felt herself flush from the sudden passion this man had drawn her into. Her temperature rose as they became more entwined. She reached behind him to feel his rear even as he was giving hers a tight squeeze. She felt her top open up and his warm tongue between her breasts. A moment of panic ensued as she glanced furtively around to verify that they were still alone, but in truth it didn't matter - she wanted him now and wouldn't stop until she had him.

The feel of his lips sucking the soft skin of her breasts made Sam throw her head back to increase the pleasure. She let out a gasp as her nipple was drawn into his mouth. Reaching down to his pants she felt his hardness, all ready for her. Her hand slipped beneath his belt and was greeted by his warm cock, responding to her touch.

Rose in Bloom

She slowly stroked him, his pants growing tighter by the second.

When there was no more room Sam lifted her hand out of his pants and deftly drew down his zipper. Pushing his underwear aside she dropped to her knees and took his shaft into her mouth. Running her tongue along the entire length she watched it jump as she hit his sensitive spots. After a while it was at maximum attention and time for her to enjoy it more thoroughly.

Jumping up on the bar, Sam slid her own pants down around her ankles. She kept them on in case she had to dress quickly, but he got the idea and bent down beneath, rising up between her legs. He paused momentarily to run his tongue over her moistness, which elicited a satisfied "Mmmmmm..." from him and a moan of delight from Sam. He was quite good there between her legs, nibbling her and sucking on her lips in just the right way, but Sam wanted more. She put her arms under his shoulders and motioned him up to her, to which he eagerly responded.

A smile crossed both of their faces as he eased inside her. Sam loved the feeling of her lips parting to accept him for the first time and then her legs widening to accept the entire thing. She brought his lips to hers again and their tongues played together once more, filling Sam's mouth with the sweet taste of her own juice. She urged him to go faster since she knew they wouldn't have much time alone. He eagerly complied of course, and Sam lay back on the bar to let him in deeper.

One of his hands wrapped around her breast, softly massaging it and playing with her nipple. The other slipped between them and his fingers found the tip of her clit. Sam couldn't believe how excited this was making her; fucking a man she had just met, in public on top of her own bar no less! She egged him on, whispering how she wanted him to fill her up with his hot cum and how he was making her burn with desire. Soon enough she was feeling exactly that as his pace quickened. His fingers kept time and soon Sam was helpless to the orgasm that started rolling through her body. With a loud moan and a shudder she came, then immediately after heard him do the same and felt her pussy heat up as he came inside her.

A few minutes later they both came to their senses and got down from the bar, now a sticky testament to their lovemaking. Sam finished getting dressed and looked up at the clock intoning with a giggle, "Closing time. I hope your evening was satisfactory sir." "Oh yes, more than I would have thought possible. I think I might just have to return here again some time to enjoy the pleasant...ummm...company," he said, as he winked at her and headed out the door.

Sam quickly cleaned up and headed out, hoping that there had been no evidence left behind. Funny how not so long ago she would have been shocked at anyone behaving like this, but now she not only accepted it, she reveled in it. She couldn't wait to get home to write this into her journal.

> *Journal, can you keep a secret? Of course you can, that's why I love you so much. I won't tell you exactly what happened but suffice to say I did some decidedly un-Samantha like things tonight. The thing is that even though it's worlds different from my normal behavior it feels so comfortable, like it was who I've been all along.*

Sometimes this big change in me is frightening though. It's almost like I'm losing my identity since everything I thought I was, I'm not anymore. I'm heading out into a brave new world and I'm loving every minute of it. I'm hoping that I at least have enough common sense to know when enough is enough, but I don't know how to tell the difference any more things have changed so much.

I guess sometimes when life flies by all you can do is trust your instincts and hang on for the ride. That's what I'll be doing, and it might lead to some more interesting conversations, but for now I'll have to leave you with that. Talk to you soon!

Back to School

The two friendly girls in her class, Vicki and Kim, had taken Sam under their wing. They were her two mother hens, which was kind of odd seeing as how she was at least 10 years older than either of them. It did have its up sides though, not the least of which was having someone to party with who wouldn't look down at her or tell her to "act her age".

In her mind she was acting her age – much older than her age in fact since she considered herself to be starting over again this year. It was lucky for her that she had done extra courses in high school and taken a few night classes. All she had to do was take a few classes this year and she'd have her Bachelor's degree.

She knew that compared to those going through the full course now her knowledge wouldn't be anywhere near as deep. She also knew that her enthusiasm and maturity would more than make up for anything she might be missing. Well, maybe not so much the maturity at the moment, she would silently add to herself.

Rose in Bloom

Looking back at the start of her library career she wondered why she had ever made the decision to work instead of pursuing her dream. She knew she somehow convinced herself that working in a library was itself a form of history, but she now saw that the perceived "glamour" of that occupation was entirely in her head, manufactured to keep her safe and comfortable.

These days the only times she felt safe and comfortable were when she was out raising hell with the girls or giving her professors trouble by asking penetrating questions. Every chance she could get she would be weaving tales about her vision of the future – how she would spend her days digging through ancient ruins and her nights in deep study of how the people of the past lived. The energy she had been able to bring forth was nothing short of remarkable, and she saw it in the increased attention she was getting from members of the opposite sex.

More and more though she had come to think of the "men" in her life (mere boys really) as a pleasant diversion rather than deep or equal partners and Tom was no exception. It was a typical Friday night, with Vicki and Kim dragging her out to a bar to party (yeah right, them dragging me…from behind as I race ahead).

Sam felt no guilt at going out this one night a week. Friday night was the choice shift at the bar so it usually went to the more experienced bartenders. She always finished her assignments the day she got them, usually before she even left the campus. In short, she had nothing better to do and it was always a good time.

At the moment their preferred venue was a dance club called Satin. Despite the name it usually attracted the jeans and leather crowd and it was always packed.

Vicki and Kim preferred to flutter around from man to man in pursuit of the evening's conquest. Sam normally just sat by the bar, and usually had better luck. Something about her new aura of confidence seemed to drive men towards her - so much so that she found she could be quite fussy about whom she chose to spend time, and share a bed, with.

This evening however Kim's mojo must have been working full strength. Returning to the table where Sam had stationed herself, Kim had not one, not two, but three delicious men in tow.

"This is Sam, my poor lonely friend I was telling you about," Kim said to the men. "One of you guys can really do me a favor by inviting her to dance."

It was Tom who took advantage of Kim's request. Sam recognized him, having seen him across the dance floor a few times. He stepped right up to her and kissed her hand. "Enchantez, Mademoiselle."

Sam's bullshit detector went off immediately and she decided to give him a little test. "A qu'elle heure êtes-vous arrivez monsieur?" She had picked up a little bit of several languages in her library stint, French being one of them.

"J'arrive a neuf heures, mon petite chou."

Sam giggled a little at his high-school french. He was a little corny but at least he wasn't one of those guys who put on a fake accent in hopes of impressing the women, but really knew no more than "Bonjour" and "Voulez-vous couchez avec moi?".

"Dancez?" she continued, accepting Kim's implied invitation to take one of them and take a hike. Guess she didn't think she could handle all three, Sam laughed to herself.

Tom was quite an accomplished dancer. He didn't look very polished but he had an extremely good sense of rhythm. No doubt he spent a lot of time here. Sam idly wondered how many women he had picked up this way, but then she realized if that were his aim he never would have had any time to learn how to dance. He was handsome enough to get a woman whenever he pleased so clearly he did enjoy the dancing.

Glancing back at her former table Sam noted that it was now vacant and both Kim and Vicki were gone. Just poor old lonely Sam left now, she said, chuckling quietly at her own joke.

She briefly wondered if they had left with the men or just on their own. On occasion over a few drinks the three of them had become "physically friendly", as Sam liked to think of it. They had touched each other and watched how they each liked to pleasure themselves. It never went any further than that but Sam often suspected that Vicki and Kim did engage in a lot more intense activities when she was not around. Sam certainly understood the allure of it, having been tempted by the closeness of their bodies at times, but hadn't decided that she wanted to do that kind of thing just yet.

All this was going through her mind as her eyes focused on Tom's movements on the dance floor. Not only was his rhythm good, so was his range of motion. His hips could do things she could only remember being able to do. It wasn't long before her thoughts turned to having him demonstrate some of those moves in a more private setting.

Not being shy to voice her desires anymore she leaned in close so that he could hear her and described exactly what she had just been thinking. She didn't even need to hear his answer; she could see it in the smile that crept over his face.

As soon as she knew he understood exactly what she wanted she turned on her heels and raced towards the door. Tom paused momentarily, wondering just what she was doing but wasn't about to be left behind. He quickly followed, arriving at the door, jacket in hand, before Sam could disappear into the night.

"Hey, wait up! What's your hurry?" he called after her.

"If you have to ask that, maybe you shouldn't be following me," she taunted back to him.

He proved faster than Sam and quickly overtook her. Putting his hand on her shoulder he brought her to a stop, turning her to face him. Sam's only response was to reach her arms around him and plant her lips right on his, holding him for several seconds in a tight embrace.

Just as he was starting to respond she broke it off and raced out down the street. Tom stood there for a few seconds again, dumbfounded at her aggression and how she seemed to so easily control him. Then dutifully he took off after her. He wasn't going to let her get away from him that easily.

In fact Sam had no idea why she was acting this way. The feelings of freedom that had been building inside her seemed to have reached some critical state and just came flowing forth. She was a tempest in a teapot, bubbling over with her own energy and now completely unable to contain it.

Rose in Bloom

She unlocked her door and jumped inside, giddily shutting it silently before Tom could race around the corner. He was faced with a corridor full of doors, knowing that one of them led to the object of his pursuit, but having no clue behind which of them his prize laid.

"Samantha, where are you?" he called out. There was no answer. "C'mon Samantha, I'm serious. I'll leave if you don't come out!"

Sam knew immediately that he was bluffing. He had wanted her before and she had only wrapped him tighter around her little finger. She felt the power she had, and was absolutely confident in it.

"This is me, walking out the door," Tom said, lowering the volume of his voice to feign walking down the hallway.

Just then he saw a piece of paper emerge from one of the doors. He unfolded it carefully and read.

QUITTER! was all it said. "So, that's your game is it?" he said through the door. "Well you'd better open the door soon or I'll start talking in a very loud voice about what I intend to do to you. Your neighbors will be shocked for days."

Another piece of paper emerged from under the door. He tugged on it and a pair of panties slid out from under the door with it - a pair of very sexy panties at that. He unfolded this second note and had a look at it.

WHAT'S THE PASSWORD? it said. Tom thought for a moment and started spewing out every possible password he could think of.

"Sam? Panties? Dancing? Tom? Bed? Lover?..." There was no reply from inside. Feeling a little frustrated he started to get a little more risqué, partially following through on his earlier threat. "Navel? Earlobes? Sweet tender neck? Soft supple breasts? Warm inviting pussy?"

Another paper emerged from under the door. This one was longer, saying **ALL YOURS IF YOU ONLY THOUGHT OF TRYING THE DOOR**. Putting his hand on the doorknob he thought, surely he hadn't been that… oh yes he had. The door opened easily. At least it was now open. He cautiously stepped inside, wondering what was there waiting for him.

He peered around the room, not seeing anyone. "Sam?" he tentatively asked. "Where are you?"

Finally he was greeted by a very loud, deliberate, and sarcastic reply coming from the bedroom. "Sheesh, it's like I have to draw you a map or something."

Tom shook his head and tossed off his shoes, heading towards the bedroom. Entering the room he was greeted by the sight of Sam lying diagonally across the bed, completely nude except for a pillow placed strategically across her midsection.

He walked over to the bed. Sam eyed him every step of the way, like a tigress ready to pounce on her prey. As soon as he was close enough that's exactly what she did. Leaping from the bed she grabbed him and pulled him back down with her. He needed no further encouragement at that point, finally starting a lovemaking session that would take them into the wee hours of the morning.

Afterwards she lay beside him, for some reason sparked to talk about her dreams. She told him her dreams and how she had quit everything to pursue them. She talked about the revelations that had come to her while thinking about her previous life, and how she had gone so far beyond that now. Through it all he sat and listened to what she was saying; or at least he appeared to be listening. But when she had finished baring her soul to him, sharing her vision all he could say was "Sounds good, can I see you again?"

Sure it was in a sexy French accent, but the content of the comment made her realize that he wasn't really listening to her at all. That is, he was listening to the words she was saying but all of the passion and emotion she had put into them, and felt about them, were completely lost on him. It was a little bit annoying, but at the same time it seemed to turn on a light bulb in Sam's head. At this point she realized that not only would she never be happy with her own life as it had been, but she would also never by happy with the shallow interactions she had dreamed about so much back then.

They continued to exchange pleasantries for a while, although Sam never let much of her intimate feelings out again after that. They even made love once more before Tom drifted off to sleep and Sam was left lying awake with her thoughts. Managing to sneak off without waking him she pulled out her journal once more.

> *Hi Journal, yeah it's me again and yes I've been doing exactly what you think I've been doing <wink>. But I think I've reached another turning point with sex. Recently as you've noticed I've devoted a lot of attention to pursuing it, and I've been pretty successful for a beginner if I do say so myself. Tonight something changed.*
>
> *Tonight I began to enjoy sex for its own sake, instead of expecting it to be this mythical earth-shattering*

experience. It was a lot of fun but that's all it was. I'm not sure if I'll enjoy it more or less now after this revelation. I do think I've grown some in learning it though.

I've also learned what kind of power I really have. I effortlessly had this guy do exactly what I wanted him to do, and enjoy doing it. I don't know what it is I have that lets me do this but it was quite exhilarating. Now Journal, I know what you're thinking. Don't worry; I won't become an evil Siren luring men to their doom. I'm still the same decent woman you met a while ago. I'm just going to have a lot more fun being me, now that I know more about who I am.

But there's a dark side to this discovery Journal. Even though sex is now just another way to have fun, I feel as if there's something more I haven't discovered yet. Like there are different types of sex and I've only just discovered that there is even one. Like a baby speaking its first word and realizing that some sounds get a pleasurable reaction. Then she later realizes that beyond words there are sentences and paragraphs; entire thoughts and epic adventures hiding in those words.

Anyway I'll keep my mind open to what might happen to me. I hope you'll be there to share my new discoveries. I'm so looking forward to them, whatever they turn out to be!

A Chance Encounter

This was the one thing Sam hated most about her school experience – the bus ride home. During the daytime she didn't mind the bus at all. It was usually a friendly place with conversations running here and there that Sam always found fascinating. People-watching was an unofficial hobby of hers and the melting pot of commuters going to work, students heading to school, and shoppers ready to catch the first sale always provided interesting distractions.

At night however it was an entirely different story. From the half-asleep late shift workers to the drunks returning home after being kicked out of their favorite watering hole there was altogether too much intensity in the gazes of these denizens of the night. Sam preferred to keep to herself on these rides and not be noticed. The long hours she kept were a burden for now, but she knew that they would pay off in the long run.

Little did she realize that on this particular ride she was being watched, albeit in a way that was entirely friendly. Philip Hunt hardly ever rode the bus, and particularly not at this time of night, but after laying eyes on Sam he was suddenly glad that he did. There was something about her – a sort of depth that seemed to lie behind her placid demeanor. He was completely fascinated by this; so much so that he found himself staring at her in a most unbecoming manner.

He watched the way she seemed to curl in on herself every time someone walked by her seat, then relax and open up like a flower blooming as they passed. At that precise instant Philip knew that he had stumbled on something special hiding in this late-night menagerie. He had to talk to her, to find out what she was really like.

But he couldn't move, so mesmerized was he by the simplest of things Sam did. She flipped her hair to the side and he felt his breath catch. She ran her fingers along her forehead and he imagined them smoothly stroking his own. She casually glanced his way and…oh god, did she notice he was staring? His heart skipped a beat – if she didn't look away he knew he would faint dead away right there on the bus. An odd sort of half-smile came to her face and she broke her gaze. She obviously saw him, but didn't think anything of it. Philip relaxed a bit.

The next evening Sam boarded the bus as usual. She spotted Philip and, recognizing him from the day before, smiled warmly in his direction. The number of friendly-looking faces on these late night rides were few and it was nice when one made a showing more than once. Philip blushed and turned his head at Sam's smile, not exactly knowing what to make of it.

The third evening Sam sat in her usual front-row seat and once again saw Philip a few rows back. Casually glancing back every so often in his direction she noticed that he's usually looking in her direction. "Well of course he is," she thought to herself. "I'm at the front, and he's probably just looking out the windshield, just as I like to do." Sam then began an internal debate with herself about whether looking out the windshield represented her desire to look towards the future, or if it was just an easy way to calm the rumbling rolling motion of the bus.

The next day brought with it the end of Sam's classes. "What a relief to be almost finished with this commute," she thought. "After the exam tomorrow I'm definitely going to go out and celebrate." Feeling a bit bolder than usual, and noticing her mysterious smiling friend on the bus once more, Sam decided to make a subtle first move and see if he's interested, or just a casual gawker. Eschewing her usual front-row seat she walked further back, taking a seat directly across the aisle from him.

Humming softly to herself Sam gazed fixedly in his direction, waiting to see what he would do. Sure enough every few minutes he glanced towards her. The motion was very subtle – just a pause in a gaze that swept from one end of the bus to the other, or a furtive glance out of the corner of his eyes, but it's unmistakable that he was watching her. The slight blush rising in his cheeks indicated to Sam that he had seen her staring back at him, but he continued his subterfuge, perhaps compelled to by some inner motivation.

Now having her suspicions confirmed Sam tried to decide what to do next. "If he's not talking to me it probably means one of two things," she pondered. "Either he's too shy to start a conversation, or he's a stalker type who is only interested in leering from a distance. Or maybe he's an undercover FBI agent keeping an eye on me to see if I'll lead him to the secret hideout of a drug lord," she chuckled to herself.

Spying her opportunity when his seatmate got off at an early stop Sam stood up and quickly occupied the now-vacant seat next to him. Turning to face him she whispered in a conspiratorial tone, "I know you've been watching me, and you know I've seen you do it. What I don't know is if you're going to continue watching or if you ever actually intend to do something about it."

He was obviously taken aback, both at Sam's forthrightness and the fact that he had now been exposed. "I'm terribly sorry miss," he began apologetically. "I really don't do things like that, but there was just something about you that kept drawing my gaze. A Siren's call if you will – I knew it might embarrass you but I just couldn't seem to resist. I hope you can forgive me."

Sam thought on this for a moment – it didn't seem like something a stalker would say; in fact his intentions seemed innocent enough and his tone of voice seemed to confirm them. Remembering what it was like to be painfully shy Sam could relate to the inner turmoil that he must have been going through and felt sympathetic.

"Well sir, unlike the Sirens of Circe I am not wont to send sailors crashing on the rocks to their doom – at least none that I'm aware of. And to my knowledge I've never turned the survivors into pigs - lord knows the world has enough of those already without my help."

Philip seemed a little more comfortable now that Sam had begun to talk to him, mentally kicking himself for not starting a conversation earlier with this obviously intelligent woman and her subtle sense of humor.

Rose in Bloom

Normally women like this terrified him but there was something in her voice and her manner that relaxed him. Almost as though he were talking with a kindred spirit.

"How clumsy of me, using such an inept metaphor," he ventured. "Especially to one as obviously intelligent and well-read as yourself."

"I **was** a librarian for many years, and you don't do that sort of job without picking up a few things here and there," Sam rejoindered. "Including such obvious and transparent attempts at flattery."

Once again Philip's cheeks flushed, not realizing what he had sounded like. "I'm sorry, I meant no disrespect. It's just that... well let's just say that the people I usually associate with are likely to think that 'Jason and the Argonauts' is a football team."

Sam had to laugh at that. She was about to reply when she looked up to see that it was her stop already. "I hate to interrupt our conversation but this is my stop."

"Will I see you again later?" Philip asked. "I'm afraid not," replied Sam. "I was taking a night school class and now I'm finished. My classmates and I are going out to celebrate tonight and cabbing it home. I won't be on this bus any longer."

"Can I call you then?" he hoped. Sam considered it for a second then answered, "I'm afraid not. A girl just can't go around giving out her number to complete strangers you know, even the handsome ones. But next time you see someone interesting in a crowd, don't be afraid to talk to them."

With that Sam stood up and left the bus, leaving Philip sitting there dumbfounded. Eventually he recovered his senses and rose to go after her, but it was too late. The bus had already started down the street again. He glanced out the window to see a sign in the distance – 'Welling School of the Arts'. That must be where her class is. Philip wracked his brain to try and remember if she had given him any clue as to what subject she was taking, but none came forth. In fact he didn't recall her even giving him her name.

Philip felt his spirits drop. He had finally been able to talk to this wonderful woman and found out that she really was someone he'd like to get to know better – and now she was gone, never to return. He was letting out a silent scream in frustration when he spotted something on the seat beside him - two somethings in fact. They were books of some kind.

The first was obviously a textbook from the University. The title suggested something in the area of Psychology but the words were unfamiliar to Philip so he couldn't hazard a guess on what exactly they were about. Besides, the second book was far more interesting.

It appeared to be some kind of notebook. It had a rough black leather cover, obviously worn from repeated use. It was a soft binding – the kind you usually find on bibles or other books meant for repeated use. He inspected the exterior, curious as to exactly what this book was. The only clue was the title on the front. Inlaid in gold leaf were the words "Thoughts" and nothing else.

Clearly his mystery woman had left this behind in her haste to exit the bus. He toyed with the idea of looking inside it to see if her name or address was there, but the foreboding nature of the title made him shy away from doing even that. "The right thing to do," he thought, "is to turn them in to the bus driver and let her pick them up at the lost and found, if they even are her books."

Even to his own ears he didn't sound convincing. He knew that what he really wanted to do was to hold onto them himself in the hopes that she would come looking for them and find him again. Then perhaps he could trade the books for a coffee with her, or even dinner! But no, that was ridiculous. Hadn't she just told him that she wouldn't be back on this bus again? "Perhaps so," he reasoned, "but maybe… just maybe these books are important enough to her that she'll check the bus one last time in hopes of finding them. The textbook may be replaceable but surely the journal must have some sort of sentimental value."

With that final thought his resolve was set. He would take the books with him then return on the bus and watch for her return to claim them. If ever there was a good reason to become a regular passenger on the bus this was it. A brief pang of regret twinged at him for doing something so devious, but that same Siren's call seemed to be forcing him down this path of action. Surely she would understand his desire to see her again and forgive this small indiscretion?

On the bus ride home that night Philip was noticeably agitated. He kept looking at every face that entered the bus, scanning for hers. He looked at every stop, thinking that perhaps she would check the bus from wherever she and her friends were out celebrating. Each stop brought disappointment though as face after face revealed nothing but uninteresting strangers (although he had to admit he did get more than his share of smiles from the ladies

– but no, his intention was clear and there was only one face in which he was interested).

Free at Last

Her final exam was now over and Sam was feeling elated. The course had been quite interesting but it was a relief to finally put it behind her. Outside of the exam room she sat and patiently waited for her friends Vicki and Kim. They would no doubt be a while yet as they seemed to have some difficulty in grasping the concepts presented during the past few weeks. Sam settled in on the small wooden bench in the hallway then pulled out her backpack. "Might as well sort through this old junk while I have the chance," she thought as she rummaged through the contents of her bag.

"Apple, hairbrush, notes on a napkin," she said, enumerating each item as it was pulled out. "Old midterm, case studies, graded final paper…" she continued, noting with some small amount of pride the large red "A" that appeared on that final paper. At length she completed her task and the contents of her backpack were laid out in front of her. "Hmmm," she pondered over the stack of items. "I could have sworn I brought my textbook with me too. Oh well, it's probably sitting at home somewhere.

I was in such a rush to get out of the house after studying that I must have left it somewhere." She didn't notice her missing journal.

At last her friends emerged, looking the worse for wear. Vicki had the faintest of smiles, indicating that although she wasn't exactly pleased with the results she probably did okay. Kim on the other hand was growling audibly at the proctor who kept looking over her shoulder, the ambiguity in the questions, the fact that her pencil broke...twice, and even some small annoyance at "those brown-nosers who finished early and left the rest of us to flounder". That last comment was obviously aimed at Sam but she just smiled and laughed, replying "Maybe if *someone* had not skipped so many classes to hide behind the dorms with Billy Ginter they could have left earlier as well."

Kim blushed at that statement, not realizing how obvious she had been. Being young and inexperienced she often forgot how Sam had already been through the rush of hormones herself and knew exactly what it could do to you. She quickly tried to divert the conversation to more pleasant matters. "I think it's time to throw off these shackles and party! Gather up that junk of yours and let's get going! What are you doing anyway, packing for an expedition to Everest?"

The three women laughed and after Sam stuffed back the contents of her backpack she had decided not to part with they were off.

Later that evening Sam found herself being whirled between a seemingly endless parade of dance partners. The music was enticing, the beat was strong, and the wine was flowing freely. This was just the thing she needed to rid her of the stress that had built up over that final exam. She thought it odd that despite the fact that she was extremely confident in her own knowledge, and believed herself well prepared for the test itself, the anxiety was still there. Not wanting to drag her evening down with deep introspection she made a mental note to herself to explore that idea more in her journal when she returned home.

It wasn't until the wee hours of the morning that Sam finally arrived back at her apartment. Both Kim and Vicki had left earlier, dates for the evening on their respective arms. Sam was quite comfortable remaining there alone and despite many appealing offers departed alone as well. Realizing she would be awake for a while as the natural high she was on wore off she figured it would be a good opportunity to record her thoughts and feelings on this final night in her journal.

She reached over to her nightstand but it wasn't there. Figuring it probably just fell down Sam leaned forward and peered over the edge of the bed… nothing. "That's odd," she thought. "I'm sure I left it there last night." Standing up she started rummaging through everything in the room, figuring that she might have tossed it somewhere and then covered it up. She had been quite distracted that week and it could be anywhere.

After a fruitless search of the room Sam started to panic. That journal was more than just a book of her innermost feelings – it was a record of how she had managed to turn her life around. In its leather-bound pages were all of the private thoughts on her inner turmoil and how she had overcome it during her transformation. Not to mention all of the lurid details of her sexual blossoming. It really wouldn't do to have that kind of thing turn up in a garage sale somewhere. Or worse, the internet!

Throwing a housecoat on Sam barged out of the room, determined to find her journal no matter what. In her mind she began to retrace her path from that morning. "Let's see, I got up, then picked out my clothes for the day…" – nothing in the closet. "Then I headed for my shower…" – nothing in the bathroom. "I came back to my room and dried my hair…" – still nothing in her room, but it never hurt to look twice. "Then I went to eat…" – the kitchen was empty, the dining room table was piled with books and notes she had been using to prepare for her final exam, but a search through them turned up nothing as well. "Then I went back to get my stuff…" – the bedroom remained annoyingly devoid of her journal after a third search. "Finally I left in a hurry so that I wouldn't miss the bus…" – nothing in the hall, the stairway, or by the front door.

Now out of options Sam sat down to ponder this further. While upstairs she had been doing nothing but singing to herself, downstairs she had been reading the paper. She remembered an article about her old library catching her eye. Something about how it was getting new computers… "That's it!" Sam shouted. She remembered that the article had sparked an old memory of the library and she wanted to write it down in her journal. Then she went upstairs to get it, realized what time it was, and grabbed it on her way out the door so that she could write it down before she forgot it.

"So," Sam thought, "if I took the journal with me then it's probably still in my backpack." Racing downstairs at this sudden revelation Sam grabbed her backpack without patience and threw it open, emptying the contents on to the floor. "Nothing…" she whispered to herself. "But I thought for sure… I mean I remember taking it with me to write on the bus." She slowly replaced the contents of her backpack, carefully inspecting each item before putting it back in the vague hope that her journal had slipped between something else, but alas once again she turned up empty. Zipping it shut she tossed it back onto the floor. A book dropped out of it as it landed and slid onto the floor. "What the," thought Sam. She stooped down to inspect it and discovered that the zipper on her backpack was worn on one side and even though it closed fine the weight of her book was enough to force it open again.

A cold chill ran down Sam's spine as she realized what must have happened. At some point during her trip or at school the pack must have opened this way and her journal fell out. Remembering her missing textbook Sam came to the conclusion that it probably had met the same fate. The hope of finding her journal seemed fainter than ever now. It could be anywhere between here and the school, and in fact even now some giggling sophomore might be leafing through it and reading all about Sam's life. Feeling defeated she trudged back up to bed, pulled the covers over her head, and drifted off to a restless sleep.

Decision

Philip was wrestling with his dilemma. On the one hand he could open the book up and try to find some clues as to who his mystery woman was so that he could find her and return the book. On the other hand it clearly contained very personal and private information and he didn't want to violate that. In the end he decided that it would probably be safe to peek inside the front and back covers to see if there was any identifying information. Gingerly he took hold of the soft leather between his thumb and forefinger, and taking a deep breath he slowly pulled it open.

Blank pages greeted him – the inside filler pages. Dare he continue on? Putting his index finger to the upper right corner he pulled down, the page responding to his touch and folding back for him, revealing itself. There it was! There was her name, as clear as day! It was a soft, sloping kind of writing, obviously that of a woman, very neatly lined up and evenly spaced. Philip read the name over several times just to make sure he had it right, then quickly shut the book to avoid the temptation of continuing to leaf through it.

He took out his wallet and wrote the name down before he forgot. Well Miss Samantha Sinclair, he thought to himself. Looks like you'll be getting your books back after all. With that he headed to the phone book to look her up. He didn't yet know if he possessed the courage to actually call her once he had the number but looking it up was something he could easily do.

Pulling the phone book in front of him Philip started leafing through the names. "Salvador…Seneca… Silberry…aha, Sinclair." There were about a dozen listings under the last name of "Sinclair" but after scanning through them Philip was disheartened to discover that there was no "Samantha", nor even an "S". This could mean one of two things. Either she wasn't listed at all, or the phone wasn't listed under her name. Philip briefly entertained the idea that she was an independent rebel who had no phone at all, but quickly put it aside as unlikely.

Long moments passed as Philip pondered what his next course of action should be. He could call all of the Sinclairs in the book and ask for Samantha on the chance that the phone was listed under her parents or, he suddenly thought with disappointment, her husband. He strained his memory to see if he could recall whether she was wearing a ring or not, but it was no use. That kind of detail was long forgotten; overwhelmed by the intensity of her mere presence.

Not having any other options Philip decided that he would in fact call every name on the list. He boldly brought the phone forward and dialed the first number before apprehension could stall his actions. "Hello," said the voice on the other end. Moment of panic – it was deep and definitely male. Quickly regaining composure Philip inquired, "Hello I'm looking for Samantha Sinclair?" "Sorry, nobody here by that name," answered the voice and the phone line disconnected.

"Well that wasn't too painful at all," thought Philip, crossing the first name off the list. One by one he worked his way through the list until finally he reached the bottom with not much to show for his work. Ten negative responses and two answering machines; neither of which had the voice of his mystery woman on them. He wrote the three remaining numbers down and put the phone book away, then pondered what his next step might be, presuming those numbers would not turn up Samantha either.

Relaxing at last

Sam turned the hot water a little higher as she generously sprinkled the bubble bath confetti into the tub. This was her idea of a real celebration. Going out to party was nice and all but relaxation could only be found by soaking in a steaming hot tub, surrounded by a mountain of bubbles. One by one she lit the candles that surrounded it then turned the lights off. It gave the room that soft, romantic glow that Sam enjoyed so much.

Even though the past months had taught her to be comfortable with her body and her sexuality, almost aggressive even, she still preferred the occasional night at home with herself and her thoughts. Maybe it was her long time at the library, but there was something about the quiet that seemed to stimulate her and, paradoxically enough, relax her at the same time.

Turning to her CD player she pressed the silver "Play" button and was rewarded by the soft strains of Bach. Although she would have preferred complete silence the background noise of the city necessitated this small concession. It was nice music for relaxing as well – slow and majestic. Sam set the volume just loud enough to drown out the small bit of street noise intruding through her window.

Looking into the mirror Sam saw herself in a way she had not seen before. The completion of her studies had given her a new kind of confidence that seemed to radiate through her body. Dropping her robe to the floor she studied the curves and lines of her form. It almost seemed like she was holding herself a little more upright – a firmer posture perhaps, brought on by the knowledge, now confirmed, that she could do anything she set her mind to. It was a heady feeling and Sam couldn't help but smile widely at the thought.

Turning, she stepped gingerly into the tub. The water was still a little hot but she knew she would soon get used to it. She preferred it a little on the hot side – it was more relaxing that way. Sliding back in the tub she gradually submerged herself until only her head was sticking above the water, surrounded by the delicately scented bubbles.

It was a gloriously decadent feeling. It was as though the ties of the world had slipped loose and she was floating outside of it all in her own little warm cocoon. As her relaxation deepened she slowly stroked her leg with her thumb. It was as much motion as she could muster at the time, and it was soothing.

Gradually the rest of her fingers joined in this rhythmic motion, running themselves softly along her thighs. The music seemed to heighten as she did so, spurring her on to move her hands in ever-widening circles. Tracing the lines of her ribs with her fingertips Sam worked her way upwards, absently counting them as she did so. "One rib… Two ribs… Three ribs…" When she reached the sixth rib she shivered as her thumb brushed lightly beneath her breast. It felt good so she continued for a while, then let the rest of her hand float upwards so that she was now cupping her breast and lightly stroking the underside with her pinkie.

It was an odd but pleasant sensation. The water gave her breasts a buoyancy that made them feel lighter and free, but her hands were keeping them in place with the softest of touches. It almost seemed like the peaks of her nipples were not a part of her body, but floating in front of her unattached, yet each touch of them electrified her.

She reveled in this sensation as one hand continued to provide it while the other was sliding downwards, seemingly acting on its own will. Sam rose to press against it as it passed her navel, wanting to feel it tightly against her but at the same time trying not to interrupt its journey to its ultimate destination.

As the tips of her fingers passed below her waistline Sam heard a low moan escape from her lips. Using what little self-control she had remaining she parted her fingers so that they slid down either side on the folds where her thighs met. She went just far enough down to feel the palm of her hand pressing against her pubic crest and then stopped.

Slowly and carefully Sam swayed her hips around. She moved in tiny little circles so as not to disturb the water, yet still enough for a tingling sensation to begin between her legs. She enjoyed this sensation most of all. It was a low pulsing that came from deep within her; almost as though she could feel her heartbeat rising to the surface in a most pleasurable way.

It was time now. Sam felt the wave rising inside her and knew she had to respond to its call. First one finger, then the other, slipped to the recesses between her legs as she parted them slightly to allow easy entrance. She shuddered as they curled up inside her, reaching up and pressing down at the same time. She raised her hips up slightly to hold tightly against her hand as the first shudder of orgasm arrived. Her fingers flicked up and down inside her as each wave of her orgasm rolled through her body. She felt it starting from her shoulders, submerging under the water through her chest and deep into her belly, then finally emanating down and out her toes. Her hand being planted firmly between her legs seemed to hold the fire in place until finally she could hold it no longer. The tremors in her hand were driving her past the point of orgasm right into pure ticklishness. "Whomever came up with the silly notion that you can't tickle yourself," she thought, "has obviously never given themselves a really satisfying orgasm."

With that Sam laid back in the tub, submerging her entire body, suffusing it with warmth. She hid in the bubbles like a rabbit hunkering down in the snow for protection. Closing her eyes she felt every last bit of tension drain from her as the soft strains of music faded away.

Pursuit

Stepping onto the bus Philip took his usual seat by the window. He spent the entire trip staring out the window, trying to think of some way he could track down his mystery woman. Keep riding the bus and hope she turns up? No, that could take weeks or months if it worked at all. Take out an ad? …possibly, but what kind of ad, and where? Call the remaining three numbers? Of course, but it was doubtful they would turn up anything. Try to find her at that school? No, she said she was finished there, why would she go back? Hmmmm, on the other hand… if she was a student there recently they would have her record on file so they know where she lives!

Philip felt excited at this revelation; so much so that he decided he would pursue it immediately. His job wouldn't miss him this one time, and he really wanted to find her before her trail went cold. Or worse, she moved far away to pursue her new career. What was it she was studying again? "Drat, can't remember," he complained to himself. "And that would have been useful information."

The bus pulled up near the school and Philip leapt from his seat, stopping the driver before he could close the door and be on his way. "I can get back on for the rest of the trip later, right?" he asked. "Sure can," the driver responded, "but it has to be today." Nodding his thanks to the driver Philip descended the stairs and headed towards what he imagined was the administrative building.

It was clearly an old school; weatherworn bricks adorned the single-pane drafty windows. There was ivy that had probably once flourished but now was reduced to patches here and there. The paint on the signs was in obvious need of attention. The irony of a School of the Arts having such a poorly attended sign gave Philip cause to grin. Despite the ivy on the walls this was obviously no Ivy League school. Inwardly this made Philip a little calmer since it would be easy to approach people working in a place like this. If he had to venture into Harvard or Princeton he might have fainted dead away.

Sure enough this was an administration building, as he noted by the large office registry posted in the front entrance. He scanned the list for anything that looked likely… Dean's Office, no, First Aid, no, Alumni Affairs, no, Lost and Found… hmmm, definitely not – they would just take it from him, unless he wanted to hang out here to see if she showed up to claim it? No, that was bordering on crazy. Office of Admissions, Room 402; that must be the one!

Pressing the elevator button Philip waited patiently, whistling to himself and a little bit giddy at the prospect of being able to find this "Samantha" at last. He stepped onto the elevator, greeted by a few odd smiles as people brushed past him and his tuneful whistle.

The elevator door opened and revealed a small reception area labeled "Student Admissions". This looked like the right place so he approached the receptionist with his question. "Hi there, my name is Philip Hunt and I wonder if you could help me?"

The receptionist looked up at him wearily. She was an older woman with slightly graying hair. Even though she was smiling politely it was obvious to Philip that she would rather be someplace else at the moment; still he pressed on. "I'm looking for a friend of mine, a student. Her name is Samantha Sinclair and I have some of her property I'd like to return to her." There, he hadn't even had to lie about it, and it seemed a perfectly reasonable request.

"Certainly sir," the receptionist answered in a well-practiced monotone. "Just leave it with me and I'll be sure she gets it."

He had counted on this and shot back "While I'm sure you would do just that I'd rather deliver it myself. It's of a personal nature and I think she'd prefer I give it to her directly. If you could just provide her address or phone number I'll contact her and arrange for just that." Whew, edging into that shady 'almost-lie' area now – he only hoped she'd prefer it, but in reality she might think him odd for doing so.

"I'm terribly sorry sir but school policy is to not give out any student's personal information. You'll have to leave it with me." This receptionist was beginning to annoy him. Still, she was only doing her job, so he had to give it one last shot.

"How about if you contact her and I wait here for her and deliver it when she arrives? Would that be okay?" Philip didn't see how she could refuse this simple request.

"I don't think that would be appropriate sir, you'll just have to leave it here with us and we'll be sure to get it to her." This pretty much cut off further discussion on the issue. Philip panicked somewhat – if he left it here he would never see her again, but if he didn't he couldn't find her. Finally he decided that a slim chance was better than none, turned on his heels and marched out of the office.

"Wait, you have to leave that here," he heard the receptionist saying in the distance as the elevator door snapped shut on what he thought had been a sure way to find his mystery woman. Arriving at the lobby he walked briskly out the door, imagining the receptionist chasing him down to get back the precious journal. Nothing of the sort happened of course but Philip was still jittery from this temporary obstacle. He sat at the bus stop patiently, thinking furiously to figure out what his next move should be.

He spent the rest of the day in a distracted stupor, blithely going through the motions of his job while his mind turned his problem over and over. The end of the day arrived and he still had nothing. Even his bus ride home offered no solace. Instead of expectantly scanning each passenger for signs of this "Samantha" he was engrossed with his own thoughts. Finally arriving at home he slipped quietly through the doorway knowing there was only one possibility; he had to look in the journal to find clues as to where she might be. He hated the thought of it; especially knowing that it wasn't even a sure thing, but he could see no other options, and he knew time was of the essence.

He laid the journal down on the coffee table as he went about preparing dinner. Several times he walked over to it, looked down at it, then decided against doing anything and walked back to the kitchen. It seemed to glare at him accusingly as he eyed it while eating; as if it knew what he was planning to do. Finishing dinner he took his dishes back out to the kitchen and sat down on the couch with a hot chocolate, trying to work up the nerve to do what he must.

Philip looked around the room, hoping for some distraction that would take his mind off this book. No such luck; everything was neat and tidy, as he always kept it. The only thing taking his attention was the ticking of the clock, now magnified into a thunderous cacophony as he tried desperately to escape from his dilemma.

In the end of course it was no use. He still had no alternative, so he tentatively reached out for the book, slid his index finger somewhere near the back and flipped it open.

The page was blank. All of that stress and there was a blank page looking at him. Of course it's blank you idiot, he chided to himself. Who would carry around a **full** journal? Reaching forward again he picked a spot about halfway through this time and slowly turned the pages back. There was indeed writing on this page. He jumped back as though bitten. Philip found himself just far enough away now so that he could see the smooth free-flowing blue ink on the page but could not make out the individual words. Straining his eyes he tried hard to see as much as possible, which was silly since all he had to do was lean forward and everything would be perfectly legible.

Oh why couldn't she have a doctor's handwriting? he lamented, still obviously chastising himself for having the nerve to even open the journal. Still, there it was; the naked thoughts of a woman he barely knew, exposed for him to see. Unconsciously he was inching forward, until he suddenly realized that it could all be seen now. He glanced casually down the page and read:

> *...barely remember that mousy girl I was last year. Meeting David in the library was the best thing that ever happened to me. I still can't believe I wasted my life working there for so many years. "Ms. S. Sinclair, Assistant Librarian, Westchester Central Library, History and Science wing." It sounds so pompous and yet I remember being so proud of that title. Still I haven't been able to replace the sense of security and warmth I had from being the master of my own, albeit tiny, little kingdom...*

That was enough for Philip, so he slammed the book shut. He knew where Westchester Library was, and logically since this entry was among the last of her entries she must have only recently left. There must be someone there who remembers her, or still sees her and knows how to contact her. With that Philip made up his mind to visit that library the next day. He stood up and grabbed the phone, calling on his friend John who normally worked the night shift to trade for the day. It would mean working a double shift the next day to make up for it but if he could get the information he wanted it would be well worth it.

Return to the Library

After a fitful night's sleep Philip got himself ready to go. Everything seemed preternaturally quiet that morning, as if foreboding a disastrous result to his trip. Even the birds had seemed to stop their twittering. Of course nothing at all had changed. It was only Philip's nervousness and lack of sleep that dulled his senses to what was going on around him. The short walk to the bus stop seemed to help a bit and by the time the bus was on its way he felt mostly awake and alive again.

Fortunately the library was only a short trip away and he arrived in short order. Stepping slowly off the bus he gingerly ascended into the entrance and turned the knob.

The library was not very busy, which only added to his apprehension. Steeling his nerves he walked towards the information desk. The petite brunette behind the desk was the picture-perfect librarian – hair in a severe bun, glasses sitting low for reading, and wearing a plain functional outfit. She glanced up as he approached, a nervous little smile crossing her face.

"How may I help you?" she asked. She seemed a little uncomfortable, although Philip couldn't imagine why. Librarian or not she was at the information desk after all and must be used to talking with people on a regular basis. Her nervousness outweighed his own at least so he was able to get his question out without stumbling over his own words.

"Yes, I'm looking for Miss Samantha Sinclair. I believe she works here?"

A puzzled look came across the woman's face. "Why she hasn't worked here in quite a while. Is there something … I … might help you with instead?" Philip noticed the unmistakable pause in her sentence. This woman was attracted to him – no wonder she had been so nervous. Taking a deeper look at her he noticed that despite the stern no-nonsense façade she was quite attractive herself. His thoughts briefly flitted away, imagining her hair hanging down loose and free over a colorful peasant blouse, her emerald eyes staring into his.

He continued to gaze into her eyes until suddenly realizing that he had been daydreaming and she was looking at him expectantly for some kind of response.

"Oh, ummm… I'm not sure about that. You see I have something of hers that I'd like to return." His thoughts continued to wander – something about those eyes…

"I'm so sorry," she responded. "But Sam didn't leave a forwarding address or any way to contact her when she left and we haven't heard a word from her since."

Without thinking Philip heard himself saying, "This is kind of an odd request, but it's really important that I find her. Um, you seem like you knew her fairly well.

Rose in Bloom

Would it be presumptuous of me to ask you out for a coffee to talk about it?"

Obviously taken aback at the question her defenses went up and she retorted, "I'm not really in the habit of going out with strange men. We haven't even been introduced." Part of her mind was shouting at her mouth to shut up but it came out anyway. A slight flush rose to her cheeks, her own words having embarrassed her.

"I have been called strange before, but only by those who know me," Philip grinned. "As for introductions I can cure that right now. My name is Philip, and by your nametag I gather that your name is Jane. Pleased to meet you Jane," he said and placed his hand out for her to shake.

It was hard to argue with the force of his conviction so Jane reached out and shook his hand, meekly replying, "Nice to meet you as well Philip. I guess my excuse for not going out with you doesn't apply any more. Oops, I didn't mean 'going out' going out, just 'going out for coffee' going out. 'Going out' going out isn't what you were asking at all was it. Was it?"

After a few seconds to parse what she was saying Philip calmly responded "Not just yet. A coffee would be good for now, if you're free."

The flush in Jane's face deepened as she realized how she'd been babbling on and what she said. All of a sudden going somewhere, anywhere, seemed like a really good idea, if only to escape the embarrassment of the situation. She picked up the phone and dialed a few digits. "Trudy? Can you cover for me for a bit? I'm taking a break."

She then turned back to Philip to confirm the plans. "Someone will be right over to take my spot and then you can buy me that coffee."

A few seconds later Jane's replacement arrived and sat down in her spot. Jane grabbed her purse and left with Philip, not saying a word. Let her wonder, thought Jane.

The two of them sat down at a small table in the corner after picking up their coffee orders. There Philip laid out his whole story, minus the real reason for his search of course. No sense in telling a stranger how he had fallen completely in love with this woman he had only briefly talked with. Still at the end Jane was impressed.

"You mean you've been searching all over for Sam just to return her book? That is so unbelievably sweet. I didn't know men like you existed in the world."

Philip grinned at the obvious compliment. It was something he had heard often but he always appreciated it. The odd thing was that it wasn't something he did on purpose. It just never occurred to him to treat others with anything but the utmost in respect, although he secretly admitted to himself that if Sam had been a middle-aged man he probably would have given up his quest at the school.

"Thank you Jane," he smiled back at her. "We nice guys always like to hear that we're appreciated." He chuckled at his comment, which was delivered without a trace of ego.

Jane leaned close to him and whispered in what she imagined was a conspiratorial voice, "You don't have a twin brother looking for a girlfriend do you?" Her eyes widened as her hand flew to her mouth, realizing the

Rose in Bloom

implication behind the comment. It was so unlike her to be this forward.

Leaning in to her in return Philip replied, "Why yes I do, and did I tell you that I'm the evil twin?"

Jane smiled, but the nearness if this desirable man was too much for her. Shifting forward ever so slightly she brought her lips up to his and brushed against them. Philip put up no resistance and returned her kiss, feeling his own temperature rise at her touch.

Slowly they separated and backed down into their seats. They sat in silence for a moment, each trying to figure out exactly what had just happened between them. Their eyes met again and held together. Philip's hand reached out and enfolded Jane's. It was warm but trembling slightly.

Philip was the first to break the silence. "You seem nervous about something."

After a short pause Jane replied, "It's just that, well, this is silly but I haven't had a kiss like that in such a long time. It made me feel like a schoolgirl again." She felt a blush rise through her cheeks.

Holding her gaze Philip smiled and said, "Maybe we should try again; now that you're used to it and all."

"Yes, I think I can agree to that," was all Jane could manage as she leaned forward to meet Philip once again. Her lips tingled as they joined with his. As their kiss deepened the tingling sensation started to spread through her face and outwards. "Oh…" she started, but could say no more.

For the moment they were both glad they had selected a corner table; it kept the stares to a minimum. Their lips parted once more but they stayed close, each only able to see the eyes of the other. Philip looked deep to see the longing Jane was feeling. There was a spark there but something was missing. He hesitated, not knowing what to say next.

"It's okay, I understand what you're thinking," Jane said, which returned Philip's attention to her. "I study people, which isn't hard really considering where I work. They come in every day looking for something and I help them find it. Eventually I could tell what someone needed just by looking at the expression on their face. You kind of have to at an information desk you know; people can never seem to explain exactly what they're after, only vague details."

She paused for a moment, weighing what she was about to say next. Philip waited for her to continue, his curiosity piqued. "You find yourself attracted to me, yet don't want to give up on this romantic quest of yours to find Sam. So how about this; we finish up this coffee at my place around the corner and see what happens from there, no strings attached. I'm not so naïve as to think one little kiss means a commitment of any kind. But it has been a very long time, and that was a nice kiss. Not to put any pressure on you or anything but I can't help thinking that what follows it will be equally nice, and even if we never see each other again I would consider the afternoon worth it."

The expression on Philip's face had not changed even though he was positively flabbergasted at this woman's forwardness. Not only that but she had managed to put into words exactly what had been running around through his head, which of course made her even more attractive. He studied her face for a long moment, looking for the slightest hint of sarcasm or humor, but none was to be found. She was dead serious about this and Philip found the whole situation terribly exciting.

Finally standing up Philip said, "I guess I'm done with mine then, how about you?"

Jane smiled and rose with him replying, "I'm done too, for the moment. Let's go." With that she offered Philip her arm, which he obligingly took, and headed out the door.

Unexpected Visit

Around the corner in the library Trudy's eyes widened as she gushed at the woman who had just walked in, "Sam!! It's so great to see you again, how have you been? Oh we've missed you here, things just haven't been the same! How did the schoolwork go? Did you land your dream job yet? What about…"

"Slow down, slow down Trudy," interrupted Sam. "One question at a time here, you're going to make me feel like I'm getting the third degree."

Blushing slightly Trudy calmed down and replied, "Sorry Sam, it's just that we haven't seen you in months and here you are out of the blue! I'm so happy you dropped by."

"Thanks Trudy, I couldn't just forget you guys, not after everything we've been through. It was hard leaving here but the school was fantastic. It's opened up a whole new world for me. I haven't actually landed a job yet but I have a bunch of good leads. I was actually in this area checking one of them out so I just had to drop in. So how are things here? Is Jane around?"

Rose in Bloom

Trudy chuckled, "Well you know the library – things are always happening. Just last week we had three best-selling authors to do readings from their books – and popular ones too, not the obscure academic titles. You just missed Jane though. She stepped out with a gorgeous guy. I'm sitting in for her while she's out. Are you here for long? She didn't say when she'd be getting back but knowing her it won't be long."

"No unfortunately, I can only stay a few minutes then I have to get on with the job hunt. Catch me up on all the latest gossip at least. Is old man McCready still sneaking peeks at the National Geographics?" she chuckled.

The two women were soon lost in a series of old memories and stories, chatting happily away for almost an hour before Sam looked down at her watch. "Oh my gosh look at the time! Sorry Trudy but I have to run, it's been great catching up with you. I promise I'll drop by again soon. Give Jane a hug for me!" With that the two embraced and Sam started out the door.

Something that Trudy said jogged a pleasant memory in Sam. Her thoughts drifted back to when she was still in the library and a handsome man had caught her interest. It seemed like a lifetime ago, and in fact it was, since at that point her life had completely changed. She vividly remembered writing all about that experience in her journal; each thought and feeling carefully recorded for posterity. With that memory a vague sadness struck her. That journal had been lost, and along with it those memories. She decided on the spot to get a new one and begin writing again. After all this was kind of the beginning of a new chapter of her life, a new journal would be fitting.

E.J. Swanson

Afternoon Interlude

Jane entered first with Philip in tow close behind her. The walk to her apartment was short and silent. Philip half expected her to change her mind and dash back to the library at any moment, so quiet and submissive she had been.

No sooner had the door closed behind him than Philip found himself suddenly engulfed in Jane's arms. She had fairly leapt upon him, now squeezing him tight and pressing her lips to his. Nope, no doubt at all what she wants, thought Philip as the last vestige of uncertainty drained from his mind.

Catching his footing Philip wrapped his arms around Jane and they clutched each other. She wasn't satisfied with that though. As Philip enjoyed the feel of her lips on his Jane was fast at work untucking his shirt, then stepping back she swept it back up over his head and tossed it to one side.

Their embrace resumed. Philip took the hint and slipped his hands into the skirt waistband, pulling her blouse upwards. It was buttoned high up though so he had to reach up to undo each button. His hands ran up from her waist, stroking her sides and chest as they rose. Slowly he loosened each button until Jane lost patience with him, finished the last button herself and flung her shirt over to his.

The lace bra she wore caught Philip's eye. It was not at all what he had expected from an information desk librarian. Something plain white with no decoration would not have surprised him. This scarlet red frilly bit of lingerie did. The barest hint of nipple was peeking over top of the left side, but the lace was so coarsely netted anyway both were clearly visible through the front.

While he was taking in the sight of Jane's chest she had not been idle. He suddenly became very aware of her warm hand sliding past his loose pants inside his boxers, grasping him gently and stroking slowly up and down.

Taking a chance Philip reached behind Jane's back and performed a deft flick with his fingers. The sudden slack in her bra rewarded him as it fell away from her body. All those years of practice had paid off after all, he thought. Noticing her freedom Jane lifted her free arm up and let her bra slide down, revealing her bare breasts to him.

Wasting no time Philip lowered his mouth to her left nipple, sucking on it gently as his tongue made a swirling pattern on her breast. Her grip on him loosened and she brought her hand out momentarily to undo his pants. Within mere seconds they had dropped to the floor as well. Clearly there was no slowing this woman down so Philip decided to go with it. His hand slid into the front of her skirt and after some searching managed to find and release the clasp holding it up. Jane gave a few deft wiggles of her hips and the skirt hit the floor too.

The softness of her skin released Philip's hesitation and he found his hand reaching down inside her panties. He followed the curve of her buttocks, stroking the surface and giving it a playful squeeze when he could. Her hands were matching his, tracing out the lines and squeezing where she could. He could feel his full erection in her fingertips as she stroked back and forth. She had a very delicate touch; just enough to arouse him but not so intense as to shorten the experience.

Before she could change that he slid his hands downward, taking her panties with him. To his further surprise he saw that she had a completely shaved pubic region. By the looks of it she kept it that way all of the time too – no burns or stubble in sight. Her pussy looked as soft and smooth as the rest of her body felt, with a glistening surface that revealed her excitement.

His tongue was the first to reach her as he leaned in and savored the sight. As soon as he made contact with her she thrust her hips forward and buried his face between her legs. Philip pressed against her, letting his tongue out to slide between the folds of her lips. Jane gasped as Philip dove in with gusto, clearly savoring the smoothness of her hair-free area.

Soon she realized that this wasn't enough for her. She wanted to feel him inside her, penetrating those warm folds and pressing tightly to her. With a Herculean effort she reached down to whisper into Philip's ear. "I want you… up here… inside me… now!"

There was no mistaking the insistence in her voice and as much as he was enjoying himself Philip was more than happy to comply. His tongue slid up her lips, giving her clit one last playful nibble, then ran right up her body – past her waist, through her navel, up over her ribs, pausing once again to give each breast a little bit of attention and get her nipples standing at attention, then up past her collarbone and into her neck.

Jane giggled slightly. Her neck had always been a sensitive area. "Oho," remarked Philip, "Looks like I've found a spot to play!" "Do whatever you want there," replied Jane, "just don't make me wait any longer!"

Nibbling behind her ear Philip listened to Jane's melodious giggling for a few more seconds, waiting for the opportune moment. On a short pause between giggles, right when she was the most relaxed, Philip took her. The giggle was replaced by a low moan as Jane encouraged him, "Oh yes, it's been so long I almost forgot how good that felt."

Continuing to press his advantage Philip slid all the way inside her, while devoting the other half of his attention to her sensitive and tasty neck. He found that he could send shivers down her spine this way, something which he enjoyed immensely. She rocked forwards as he touched one particularly pleasurable spot, knocking them both backwards onto the couch, not missing a beat.

One of those shivers went on a little long as Jane's orgasm approached. Philip's mouth gently sucked on the sensitive area behind her earlobe. It was just hard enough to be a bearable tickle but not so hard as to leave a mark. The shivering turned into a hard quaking as Jane peaked, squeezing Philip tightly to her. He felt her tighten up around him completely and felt himself losing control as well. All he was aware of was the hard breathing in his ear

Rose in Bloom

as wave after wave hit Jane. Somewhere in there Philip came as well but one moment blurred into another as the two of them held each other through it all.

Philip was vaguely aware of movement around him, not quite returned to his senses after the intensity of the orgasm had subsided. He looked up to see Jane peering down at him, fully dressed and looking like she was still sitting at the library information desk.

"I expect you'll want something to drink; help yourself to anything in the fridge. Thanks for a wonderful afternoon; I really needed it. I truly hope you find Sam; she's a lucky woman to have someone like you looking for her." With that she leaned down, kissed him warmly, and left to return to the library.

Musing on his situation for a moment Philip finally arose, got dressed, and left as well. Looks like the trip to the library wasn't a total loss after all, he thought to himself.

Try and Try Again

The next day Philip resumed his familiar spot, staring at the journal and contemplating what his next move should be. Should he open it up again and read more? Should he hang around the library every day until Samantha returns? Should he give up on this fantasy world entirely and just turn the book into a lost and found somewhere?

In the end his curiosity gets the best of him and he decides he should try another page in the book. Giving it a bit more thought he reasons that the most likely place to find a good clue about how to contact her would be the most recent entry. After all, that would be the last thing she did and may contain something more revealing like her address or favorite hangout.

Stupid idea, he thought. Why would anyone write her own address in her own journal? And a favorite hangout could be anywhere in the book; the only way to tell if it was the favorite would be to count the number of times she mentions it. But that would mean reading the whole thing. Philip flinched at the mere thought of it. He was now contemplating crossing the line between a (semi-) innocent search for clues on how to return the journal and out-and-out voyeurism.

No, he would only look at the final page this time. Furthermore, he resolved to himself, if that doesn't prove to be fruitful I'll go right back to the school and have them forward it to her and it will be out of my hands.

He wasn't quite sure he could actually follow through on such a resolution but it at least eased his conscience. Gingerly he opened the journal from the back cover and started flipping forward.

Blank page… blank page… blank page… It seemed to be proceeding at an agonizingly slow pace but he didn't dare flip faster lest he miss the page he was searching for. At last he came upon a page with writing. Okay so technically it was two pages, right and left side, but he knew he'd never be able to resist reading both so he changed his own rules and assured himself that these two counted as one page to be read. Her flowery writing filled the pages quickly, and the passage was short. Starting at the top left corner he read:

> *…adventure at school is about to come to an end. One last exam and everything's done. The girls are no doubt going to try to get me out to celebrate; maybe I'll give in to them just this once since there won't be any more studying to do. I still don't think I'm ready for this last exam but I guess there's no turning back now. I'll soon find out how much I've learned at any rate. Wish me luck! Until next time, ciao.*

Damn! thought Philip as he read and reread the last page. There wasn't a single clue in there as to where she might go or what she might be doing. She might go anywhere to celebrate; the area surrounding the campus was littered with bars, dance clubs, and other nightspots, always filled with college kids blowing off steam. Or for all he knew their favorite spot might be out of town, or some male strip club.

Glancing back at the journal Philip realized that he couldn't pry into it any more. These thoughts were never meant for him and if he was to find out any more about the private life of Miss Samantha Sinclair it would be from her in person, not through a questionably obtained recording of her life. Here is the chance for Philip Hunt to show his quality, he said to himself in mock deference to the line by Faramir from *The Two Towers*. Would he stick to his self-imposed promise and look no further, giving up his quest, or would he go back on it and try to find yet more clues to the whereabouts of his mystery woman?

He thought about it for a while before realizing that he had, intentionally or not, left himself a loophole. While he had vowed to return the book to the school he didn't specify when, nor did he say he would actually give up looking before the book had been returned. It was fairly questionable reasoning to say the least but so long as he was satisfied with it nobody else was around to dispute him. The only problem then was exactly what to do next given that he at least would not look in the book itself for further information.

He pondered this problem for a long time before finally hitting on, in his own opinion, a brilliant solution.

The Poacher

The leather skin of the journal felt soft beneath Sam's fingers. She stroked it gently, the distinct aroma of newly tanned leather in the air. The shining gold clasp opened easily to her touch. She pulled open the cover and was greeted by pristine ivory colored pages with just the hint of gilding on the edges.

Dear New Journal, Sam printed neatly onto the first page. Welcome to my life! I know we've just met and all but I'm going to tell you some very private things so I hope you don't mind my forwardness. Where to start? Your predecessor was very good to me, listening patiently to my proudest, and not-so-proudest, moments. It was my friend, my confidante, and my ally in this battle called life. I hope in time we can enjoy the same friendship. Friendship is a funny word for a journal I know, but when I lost it I felt like I had lost a friend. It knew my most intimate moments, something that no other person knows so in a way it was my best and only friend for the longest time. Of course I've become much more worldly since I started it and finally have come to realize that friends are the most valuable thing you can add to your life. Still, it was the first and I'll miss it dearly.

Now that you've seen you have some fairly big shoes to fill, so to speak, let me start you off by telling you about the end of my education. Well, …

Sam continued writing for several hours more, spilling her thoughts and feelings onto paper. She recounted the past few days and all of the emotions she had been feeling as her life had reached another critical junction. Being in the middle of it Sam found it hard to reconcile exactly how much things were going to change. Now that she was writing it down the stark reality of it was hard to avoid. The sheltered little word she had enjoyed for the past year was coming to an end; now it was time to make things happen, exactly as she had planned when embarking on this life change.

Dropping the pen for a moment to rest her hand Sam looked up at the clock. She couldn't believe how long she had been writing. Until this moment she hadn't realized how much she really relied on her journal to get things off her chest. Friday night again, she sighed. It won't mean the same now that I'm out of school. Last Friday had found her partying with Kim and Vicki until the wee hours. That wasn't quite what she felt like at the moment but a little distraction might be welcome. Besides, she thought; most of the college kids will have gone home now that the semester is over anyway.

Sam threw on one of her standard Friday night outfits and strode out the door. Cabs were everywhere on Fridays so it didn't take her long to flag one down. She had always thought calling for one was less romantic than just running into the street and finding one. After

Rose in Bloom

some quick instructions to the driver they were off. What seemed like only seconds later they had arrived at The Poacher. Sam gave the driver a generous tip, as was her custom on Fridays, and went in to the bar.

As she had predicted the place was all but empty. Where normally there would be standing room only by this time, tonight found most of the tables empty. Even the bar held only a few of the regulars. Sam idly wondered if some of them only hung around here to try and pick up the college women. She had certainly been witness to that enough times to know it was pretty common.

Not wanting to be stuck at a table all by herself Sam instead broke with tradition and found an empty stool at the bar. She had often seen the regulars playing this trivia game on the screens behind the bar and been dying to try it, but Kim and Vicki always kept her too busy between the dancing and the rescuing them from some would-be suitor (or keeping one away from the other when they were particularly interested in some guy).

The bartender took her order and dropped one of the sleek electronic boxes in front of her. So many buttons; Sam didn't know what to do at first so she tried pressing a few of them just to see what happens. She giggled to herself with the thought that last year she probably would have just sat there wondering what to do, but the new Sam was more adventuresome and impatient to try things out.

Apparently she had been pressing all of the wrong buttons because nothing was happening. "Would you like some help?" came a voice from behind her. She started slightly and looked back to see one of the regulars. Brad, she thought she remembered him being called. Very easy on the eyes but always occupied with some young thing.

Well why not, she thought to herself. Who knows, maybe there's more to this boy than a cute face. "I do believe I would," she replied, explaining, "I've never played this game before but I thought I'd give it a whirl. It doesn't seem to like me though. No matter which buttons I push nothing is happening."

Brad smiled, and a very attractive smile it was. "Yeah, the interface is kind of cryptic but once you get used to it it's pretty easy to understand. The first thing you have to do is enter your name so that it knows who you are."

"It would know who I am? But," said Sam, in a surprised way. Chuckling Brad cut her off, "No not literally of course. You just enter a name for identification. It doesn't have to be your real name. Every now and then the scores flash on the screen and you can see how you're doing compared to the rest of the bar. See, there it is now," he continued, pointing to the screen behind the cash register. Sure enough there was a list of names, each incomprehensible to Sam on first glance. It looked like a list of license plates to her – GLD8OR, HOTSTF, JIMBO, and so forth.

"There's me, at number 2," he told her. The name in the #2 position on the screen was "BRADBOY". Sam smiled at the obvious pun and played along with it. "And are you? A BrADBOY that is?" she teased, with an unmistakable softening of the "R".

"Ummm…" Brad stammered, "Well my name is Brad and everyone calls me that so that's why I chose that ID." "Nice try hotshot," replied Sam. "I come here all of the time and I know that name is more descriptive than you let on." With that Sam gave him a sly little wink.

Brad looked slightly embarrassed but didn't let on in any way. "Why don't you enter a name and we can continue with our game here?" Briefly Sam wondered if she wouldn't have seen right through these obvious lines in the past. Knowing exactly what he was up to gave her a sense of power though. She didn't want to give that away just yet so she continued to play along with him. Scanning the keyboard she chose a name for herself – SAMIAM.

Brad looked at her selection and asked, "Let me guess – your name is Sam? Short for Samantha I bet." Trying not to roll her eyes Sam answered in her best singsong voice, "Right you are. But nobody calls me Samantha any more." Not too bright, she thought, but not bad company at least. She waited for him to prove her wrong but no, he hadn't caught the Dr. Seuss reference. Not much of a sense of humor either; there's only one last hope. "Say Brad," she began. "Would you like to dance?"

"Absolutely," he enthusiastically responded, jumping off his stool. "Let's go!" He took her hand and they went off to the dance floor. Sam had been listening to the music and was careful to ask when a relatively 'safe' song was playing. No slow dances just yet, and no Salsa. It was "Footloose" by Kenny Loggins, one of Sam's favorites. She began whirling and skipping across the floor to the music. It was a good choice. This song always made her feel like dancing.

Once she felt the beat and got into a rhythm all thoughts of her partner evaporated. She was in the music now and he was on his own to try to keep up with her.

From corner to corner she traveled, using most if not the entire dance floor as she skipped across. It was rare that the floor was so empty so Sam wanted to take full advantage of it. To her surprise though Brad was keeping up with her and matching her step for step. His style was a little rigid, like he had taken a few lessons but quit after learning the technique only, but he was easily better than pretty much all of the partners Sam had ever had. Not including Vicki and Kim of course, who danced in the same free uncaring way Sam had. She was pretty sure it was them who taught her everything she knew on the dance floor and at times like this she was eternally grateful. She felt the energy flowing through her, giving her strength and purpose. It seemed to cut through the social veneer and taboos and hit her right at the deepest level.

The music switched to something a little more modern and slower. Not quite in the "slow dance" category, much to Sam's relief. She didn't want to deal with the inevitable gentlemanly invitation to dance, followed by the equally inevitable roaming hands. Sam was still taking his measure and didn't want him to get that close too easily. Fortunately the new song gave her just what she wanted. It contained a little bit of shimmy and shake, with some slow sensual movement.

Brad seemed to be at home with the latter, sidling up within inches of her as the music taunted them both. Sam could hear the music egging them on, almost daring them to succumb to its temptations. Leaning back onto Brad during a particularly sultry section Sam let his hands slide down her body while she reached up and ran her fingers through his hair.

Rose in Bloom

For hours the two of them danced in this way; Brad trying to get closer and closer to her but Sam letting him get so far and then subtly but insistently moving away. She was enjoying herself immensely. This outing was exactly what she needed. The only question now was, what to do with Brad?

She was definitely enjoying his company, even though he was a little on the "intellectually challenged" side. And a few discreet brushes against him in the right place let her know that he was definitely enjoying himself as well. It was no wonder women had all of the power in deciding whether their man got any or not. You could always tell where a man stood, so to speak, but whether a woman was attracted could remain her little secret until she chose to divulge it.

As the strains of the last song faded from the speakers Sam had made up her mind. She wrapped her arms around Brad, pulled him close and planted the most sensual, warm, and inviting kiss she could manage onto his lips. Her head tilted back as she went on her tiptoes to whisper into his ear. In her sexiest Kathleen Turner voice she purred to him; "This evening has been wonderful, but I have to leave now. Maybe I'll see you here again some time."

Before he had a chance to protest Sam turned and walked smartly to the door. As she departed she looked back over her shoulder at Brad, still flabbergasted, gave him an impish smile and blew him a kiss before the door closed between them.

Oooh, Samantha you evil woman, she mock-chided herself, jumping into the nearest taxi. She gave the driver her destination and had only a few pangs of regret on the short trip home. It really hadn't bothered her to end the evening there. Although she didn't promise anything specific to Brad she knew the male mind. He would be wondering for days what he did and why he didn't get any from her. It wasn't hard for her to convince herself that he would have a new target by next week and probably wouldn't even remember her anyway.

Help Wanted

Philip was so excited he could hardly contain himself. The exhilaration of stumbling onto an idea that one was 100% confident in was a great feeling. It was rare for Philip, perfectionist that he was, to not hear a nagging doubt in the back of his head telling him the hundreds of ways this idea would fail. She wouldn't see it. She would see it but not understand it. She would understand it but not care enough to respond. Those were the criticisms any objective person would level at Philip's plan but his direction was clear.

His idea was to place an ad in the newspaper describing the lost book. But not in the lost and found, since that was a small corner of the newspaper hardly anyone looked at. He was going to place an ad in the "Help Wanted" section. Obviously the first thing Samantha would be doing after graduation is find a job for herself so, he reasoned, she would be scanning the Want Ads very carefully every day looking for that perfect job. Knowing from experience how long that might take Philip was perfectly confident that he could place it any day and she would see it.

Now to the wording - something obvious, and descriptive, but not too forward; maybe even a little romantic. He realized that it would be easy for her to take this type of gesture the wrong way, mistaking him for a stalker of some kind, and not answer. That thought stopped Philip for a moment. Wasn't he behaving in precisely that manner? Was he a stalker? Ridiculous he chided to himself. All of this politically correct nonsense wasn't going to get to him. He was a courtier in pursuit of a lady, and he was being the consummate gentleman. He had in fact been almost Victorian in some ways; keeping his distance, not prying into her personal affairs. This ad was merely the modern equivalent of arranging to accidentally bump into her at the local social.

A quick brainstorming session later he had come up with the first draft of his ad.

> **W A N T E D**
> *Sensitive, intelligent, articulate woman, recently graduated from the Welling School of the Arts. Initials SS a plus. Needed to resume guardianship of leather-bound journal left on city transit, currently in the care of P. Hunt. Apply in person at the fountain in the city square this Saturday at noon. Résumé not required.*

There, that was it. Not too formal sounding; friendly, with just a touch of silliness. And the neutral ground for meeting was a particularly nice touch. Philip decided that further editing would probably make it seem too contrived and would no doubt end up driving him crazy trying to wordsmith just the right phrasing. Without further thought he called up the newspaper and placed the ad in the next day's paper.

Rose in Bloom

Found at Last

Sam tossed the paper aside into the small pile that had been forming all week on her normally neat kitchen counter. The early morning sun spotlighted the collection she had been gathering all week, almost teasing her about her search. She knew that searching for a job would be frustrating but knowing that didn't really make it any easier. She briefly entertained the thought of returning to her old job at the library but, no, she didn't think she could do that anymore. The old Sam needed the solitude and to stay away from people, but now she craved the contact. She had become fascinated with people and how they behave, and found that she thoroughly enjoyed the company of pretty much everyone she met these days. Everyone had something unique to offer and Sam was always able to draw that out of them.

Over the past few days she had methodically traced through the Want Ads, making several passes in her search for the perfect job. She imagined it was an advantage to her that she had no particular position in mind since she had no real specialty. Unfortunately at this stage of the game that advantage meant a lot more work for her since she couldn't automatically filter out areas outside of her expertise.

The first pass was for pure interest, and usually filtered out the least number of things since she was interested in almost everything. (Must be a holdover from her library days when she would read every book she could get her hands on, no matter the topic.) The second pass was for positions she didn't really want; oil rig mechanics, CEOs, computer programmers. Either the job itself was unappealing or the environment was. The next pass was for location. The idea of a long commute was repulsive to Sam since it was the opposite of what she wanted. From her bus travels to and from school she knew that commuting meant being in a large crowd of people and interacting with none of them. That would drive her crazy after a while, so anything located in an area of town where she wouldn't live was off the list.

That always left her with her dream list, and unfortunately so far had only turned up jobs for which she was seriously under-qualified. She had sent résumés to each of them anyway, hoping that they would at least grant an interview. If she got that far she knew she could convince them she was the right person for the job, but these days most companies had well trained front-line staff that didn't let you in to see anybody except by invitation.

Sam sighed and wandered out to the front door. Today's paper should be here by now; might as well go through it too before I hit the pavement again, she thought. And there it was, leaning precariously on the edge of the front porch. Sam marveled at how the newspaper boy always managed to put the paper in a completely different location every day. At least there were no handy puddles for him to aim for today.

Walking inside she tossed everything but the Want Ads onto the couch for later perusal - business before pleasure after all. Scanning the ads quickly she filtered out the usual suspects, ditching the menial labor, the remote locations, and the mind-numbing repetitive work she despised. Sam had become an expert at sorting through the cruft in the ads and this filtering process went quickly. The next one required more attention though, as she had to actually read the entire ad to see what the job was all about.

A few were ticked here and there, one was circled to definitely look into, when she happened upon a rather odd ad. At least at first glance it looked like an ad, but on reading it Sam discovered that it was actually more like a lost and found entry. "Hmmm.. hmmm..initials SS… blah…blah..leather bound journal…blah blah…city fountain," she muttered to herself as she read it. It was kind of surreal in a way. As she read it became obvious that the ad was referring to her own missing journal, and this P. Hunt must be the person who found it. She hadn't made the connection to her seatmate on the bus, knowing him only as Philip. She was thinking it was somebody at the school who had found it, but why on earth would they choose this odd method of trying to return it.

Dozens of answers leapt to Sam's mind as she unconsciously sat about trying to solve the problem before her. It's not somebody who knew where she lived, and her phone number was unlisted so they couldn't have found her that way. The school would obviously not give

Rose in Bloom

out her address to anyone so this person with her journal must have been looking for some other way to find her - but why not the lost and found department at the school, or even in the paper? A cold chill crept down Samantha's spine as the worst thought momentarily flitted into her brain. Suppose this stranger has read her journal and knew everything about her? There were some very private thoughts in there; things that someone with malicious intent could easily use against her in some way. Was this an attempt at blackmail?

In the end Sam decided that she was being a little too paranoid about it. This must be some Good Samaritan type who was merely trying to return her lost journal to her. She felt a vague sense of admiration for this stranger, having gone to the trouble of using such a unique way of contacting her. It was certainly no secret at the school that she would be looking for work and on reflection she realized that if there were an ad in the lost and found section she never would have seen it. Her days were consumed with the job search; looking through the lost and found at school or in the paper hadn't even crossed her mind. A little bit happier now at the prospect of having her journal returned to her Sam posted a big reminder on her fridge for Saturday and then resumed the business of searching for a job.

When Saturday finally rolled around Sam was feeling a little less optimistic about her journal. Several days more of fruitless searching had left her empty-handed, with no real job leads to speak of. At least she got a few ideas of where she'd be interested in working; now it was just a matter of finding that ideal job and jumping on it.

After debating whether or not to have an early lunch Sam decided against it, opting instead to write in her new journal about the prospect of recovering her old one. It was an odd sensation; almost like telling a new husband that the old one, missing at sea for years, was returning. A silly thought she knew but that's how she had come to think of her journal over the years. Closing up her entry she grabbed her sunglasses and keys and headed out the door, hoping once more that the old journal had not been read. She almost blushed at the thought of even the most trustworthy person reading some of the entries, let alone some random person who just happened to find it.

Arriving at the fountain she didn't see anyone around who looked like they might be harboring her journal. She decided the best thing to do was to sit and wait, and let them find her. The thought suddenly occurred to her that she had been assuming it was a man who had discovered her diary. It could equally well have been a woman. Sam couldn't decide if that would be better or worse. She knew that women could be far more judgmental if given the chance, but at least some of her worries would be unnecessary.

The sun was warm on her, sitting there on the side of the fountain. She leaned back and listened to the water falling behind her. It was quite relaxing; almost musical. She listened carefully to the people passing by, as if she would be able to tell by their footsteps if they were in possession of her missing journal. Soon she heard a set approach then stop beside her. Opening up one eye behind her sunglasses she peered over at the new arrival, not giving away yet that she knew someone was there.

Rose in Bloom

A handsome man stood before her. He was tall, but not too tall, and very well dressed. He wore a beige jacket over a white collared shirt, unbuttoned where a tie might normally appear. She casually scanned him as he stood there and he was making no effort to make his presence known. Sam spotted something tucked under his arm, and with a little concentration she could make out what it was – her lost journal. This was the mysterious P. Hunt who had so cleverly contacted her, and clearly he knew her by sight since he was standing right beside her awaiting acknowledgement.

Opening both eyes and turning to face him Sam intoned, "You're late," in what she imagined was a slightly distant but still playful tone. She wondered how he would take it.

"Of course I am. I know what you look like but I doubt you'd remember me so it only made sense for me to arrive after you so that I could find you." It wasn't a very convincing excuse, but Sam sensed that it was at least sincere.

She looked more closely at him and responded, "Sure I do; you're Philip from the bus. Quite clever of you to place that ad in the paper."

Philip smiled back at her, slightly embarrassed at the compliment but glad that it had been noticed. "You have no idea what I've gone through to return this to you." He noted a sudden look of concern on Sam's face and quickly added, "Oh don't worry, I didn't look at it… well much anyway. I looked at one page just to get some clue about where to find you." His slight embarrassment deepened into a light blush as he realized he'd just confided what could be considered a major sin to Samantha.

"Obviously you looked at the wrong page then, or you would have seen my name and address in the front of the book," Sam chided. Philip mentally smacked himself on the forehead, suddenly feeling like Homer Simpson's dumber brother.

"Oops, I wish I'd thought of that. I looked at the last page to see where you might be found," he confessed, happy that she didn't seem that upset he had opened the journal. Then he realized out loud, "Wait a minute. I **did** look in the front and only your name was there!"

"That's the inside cover. My first entry was me introducing myself to the journal," Sam explained. "Name, address, phone number, hopes, dreams, aspirations – it was all there at the start. Soooo, a hunter are you? Or did you imagine yourself as a Sherlock Holmes type who could find me given only the way I drew the period at the end of my final sentence?" Sam found herself enjoying this. She was relieved that it was Philip who had found her journal. She had come to see him as fairly harmless in their brief time on the bus, and she thought herself a fairly good judge of character.

"Well you caught me," said Philip. "I just couldn't resist the chance to find you in a way that might even impress you a little bit. I can see now that I'd have to do a lot better than that to impress someone like you – you're a mile ahead of me already and I had days to think about it."

"Not to worry," chuckled Sam, "I'm sure you'll be able to think up something at Appleby's."

Philip looked at her, bewildered. "Appleby's?"

Rose in Bloom

"Yes, Appleby's. That's where I'm taking you to lunch as a reward for finding my journal. It's the very least I can do."

Although pleased to find his plan working so well Philip remained uneasy, wondering if she had seen right through him again and knew this was part of his purpose in tracking her down.

As they walked down the street towards the restaurant Sam casually said, "You didn't really look through the rest of the journal, did you". It wasn't a question; merely a confirmation of his character, which he now became a little proud of seeing it recognized this way.

"Nope, but I have to admit to you Samantha that it was awfully tempting. You obviously have a strong attachment to it so there must be a lot of really private material in there," teased Philip.

"There most certainly is," admitted Sam. "and please, call me Sam. 'Samantha' reminds me of the bad old days when I was a prissy librarian."

"Well Sam I have to admit that I don't know a lot about you but 'prissy' was never a word I would have thought of."

Arriving at the restaurant the hostess seated them at a quiet booth in the corner. Philip regaled Sam with the tale of his adventure in trying to find her. Sam had to laugh at the near misses he had had, and the thought of how frustrated he must have been.

"It's like that line from the old Batman movie," she joked. "Some days you just can't get rid of a bomb," chimed in Philip, and they both laughed.

The lunch ended all too quickly for Philip, who had been having a marvelous time with Sam (not surprising at all, he thought). He offered to throw in the tip, which Sam graciously accepted. Then he sadly added, "I guess this is the end of my grand adventure", with a half-smile on his face.

Sam looked him in the eye with a mischievous grin. "Surely you're not giving up that easily. I was hoping you'd come back to my place for a drink. I'm done job hunting for the day… unless you have some place you'd rather be…" she trailed off.

Feeling his breath taken in for a moment Philip hastened to answer, "Of.of..of course I'd like to go with you. I mean you're funny, you're intelligent, beautiful… A guy would have to be crazy to turn down that kind of invitation."

"Flatterer," replied Sam. "Well? Shall we go then?" Sam rose and offered her arm to Philip, who gladly took it and off they went. Philip couldn't help but feel he looked like a grinning idiot at this point, but he didn't care one bit.

Getting Intimate

They arrived at Sam's place still laughing at the last joke Philip made. Sam closed the door behind them and locked it. "I guess there's no escape for me now," quipped Philip. Sam only smiled in return and turned for the kitchen. Philip followed in anticipation. He didn't really know what to expect from Sam at this point. She was so self-assured that she would pretty much do whatever she felt like. But he had his hopes of course.

Sam stopped at the kitchen door and turned to face him. "Why don't you relax in the living room while I make the drinks?" she told him. Again it was unmistakably not a question, so Philip veered off towards the living room and set himself down on the couch. He heard Sam call from the kitchen.

"I hope you don't mind a fruit smoothie. They're my favorite, and I find them relaxing after I've been out all day."

"That sounds great," replied Philip, although truthfully he wasn't really sure just exactly what a 'fruit smoothie' was. It sounded good though.

Gliding gracefully into the living room Sam plopped down beside Philip, handing him his drink. He took a sip and was pleasantly surprised. "This is delicious," he said. "But of course," replied Sam, in a mock French accent. "I am ze mistress of ze smoozie. Graduated first in my class of three at ze smoozie academy."

Philip laughed again and took another sip of his drink, watching Sam dig into hers with gusto. She finished quickly then turned around. "How are you with necks?" she asked. "I've had this crick in it all morning, probably from sitting so stiffly at those interviews. I don't know what it is about them but I always get so tense."

Knowing an invitation when he heard it Philip quickly replied, "I've never had a complaint yet."

"Ahhh, that could mean you've never done it before," noted Sam.

"Why don't you be the judge then?" responded Philip, as he laid his hands on her shoulders.

"Brrrrr!" Sam yelped, jumping slightly, "Are you trying to freeze me?"

"Oops, sorry," apologized Philip. "I forgot about the cold smoothie hands." Then he playfully put his hands on her neck for a second.

"Heyyyy, you brat!" giggle Sam. "A gentleman would warm those up first."

Finally relenting Philip rubbed his hands together and blew into them to heat them up. He slipped one down the side of Sam's neck and asked, "Is that better madam?"

"Mmmmm, much better thank you. You may proceed."

Rose in Bloom

Sam felt the tension drop from her shoulders as Philip squeezed gently at the corners of her neck. His soft yet firm touch told her right away that he had some skill at this. Philip progressively squeezed a little harder and each time he did Sam felt a little knot loosen up. Every time she thought he had them all he found another. The sensation was wonderful. It was as though her shoulders were floating in warm soup, completely relaxed.

"Enough with the preliminaries," announced Philip, "now on to the main area. I hope you didn't think I was forgetting what you asked me for but I've found it's always better to loosen up the shoulders before tackling the neck."

"Mmm, feels good this way," was all Sam could muster in way of a reply. Her eyes had drooped closed as she surrendered herself to his skilled hands. It wasn't long before he was bringing the same relaxation to her neck as well. Sam shivered when she felt his fingers run across her hairline, feeling the goosebumps rise just behind his touch.

Her neck had that same floating feeling and she was only vaguely aware of him asking, "You seem to have a lot of collected tension. Do you mind if I continue?" The warm noodle that was her neck bobbed up and down in acquiescence and Philip began working his way down her back.

It was exquisite, feeling those sensitive fingers taming the wild knots that she held in her back. It was only the contrast of the already relaxed areas that made her at all aware of them. I guess I just got used to the tension, she said to herself – or was it aloud? Reality seemed to meld into her own private fantasy world now and she couldn't quite tell what was real.

So relaxed was she that her body slowly toppled sideways, caught and guided down gently by Philip's caring arms. Carefully stretching her onto the couch on her stomach he continued to work on her, kneading the knots from her tired muscles. His touch even seemed therapeutic. Sam could swear that she felt the heat flooding into her everywhere he made contact with her. He slipped off the couch so that he could reach all parts of her body.

She had to have more of his touch. Somehow managing the effort she reached up and undid her blouse, sliding it first off one arm, then the other. Her practiced hands snapped open her bra and let the straps fall to her side. The heat from his hands seemed to spread deeper now that he had contact with her bare skin. It was positively intoxicating, the way he was handling her. Somehow he managed to keep his concentration on doing exactly what would make her feel good, despite the obvious intimacy of his touch. Once or twice she felt his hands slide down her side towards her breasts but each time they stopped short and returned.

He soon moved onwards past her waist, treating her buttocks with the same attention and care as the rest of her. Sam felt a familiar stirring inside her that she knew she wouldn't be able to deny for long. She reached down to undo her skirt, hoping Philip would take the hint. Indeed he did. On his next pass down to her hips he brought her skirt with him, then continued straight down her legs, tossing her skirt to one side. He then returned

Rose in Bloom

and did the same thing with her panties, letting out an appreciative "mmmm…" as he did.

Once again Sam felt the heat flood into her from his hands, only this time it seemed to be coming in from multiple directions at once. As his hands squeezed tightly around her thighs and pulled the muscles downward Sam's desire reached critical levels. She guided his hand back up between her legs and pressed her wetness against it. Philip responded, stroking her softly and skillfully, taking his time to enjoy the sensation before slipping a finger inside her. His touch there was as enjoyable as it was everywhere else, causing Sam to let out a small gasp.

She felt Philip's hand underneath her shoulder, lifting her up, and she obediently rolled over on her back, still with her eyes closed. The slow pressing of his hand was soon replaced by something warmer, which could only be his tongue. Sam felt it dart playfully around her lips, flicking out to stimulate her for a minute then diving back down for a deeper taste. His hand had moved up to her left breast and softly squeezed the nipple, causing it to stand up in response.

As if sensing her desire his hand left her breast to reach down to his own shirt and pants. He managed to undo them and toss them aside, never breaking his lip contact with her. In one swift motion he rose up and plunged inside her. She grabbed his head and lifted up to meet him in a deep kiss. Her legs wrapped around him as they kissed, pulling him in closer.

"Oh Sam, I've dreamt about this for so long," he whispered into her ear. "I can't believe how good it feels."

"Yes Philip it feels great. Keep doing it," Sam replied, giggling slightly as he blew in her ear. Her hands dug into his back, clenching tightly as their hips rocked together at a steadily increasing pace. She heard an anxious sound from deep down his throat and knew he was trying desperately to hold back his orgasm. Squeezing him hard on each stroke Sam pressed against him to bring herself to the edge too. She threw back her head. "Don't hold back, I want to feel you cum. I want you to go deep inside me."

With her leaning back now Philip could watch her breasts sway back and forth in time with their rhythm. He dutifully obeyed Sam's command and went as far in as he could, staying there as she swirled her hips against him. Bending forward slightly he took her right nipple into his mouth, first tentatively, then sucking gently on it. He started to feel the tightness between his legs and engulfed what felt like her entire breast into his mouth.

His mouth felt good on her breast and Sam brought his hand up to her other one. She could feel the telltale signs that he was going over the edge so she did that last little swivel that would take her over with him, reveling in the pleasure she was feeling that had now spread from between her thighs to encompass her whole body. Time stood still for her. She felt every last drop of sweat between their bodies. The places where they were in contact seemed on fire while the rest of her felt the cold chill of the outside. Time froze as this moment hung in the air when the final wave of her orgasm came crashing down on her, snapping her back into reality.

They lay there for a few moments recovering their energy, holding each other not just for warmth but to

Rose in Bloom

extend the connection they had just made. Philip was the first to break the silence, smiling at Sam and joking, "So I guess you have something new to write in your journal, huh?"

Chuckling slightly Sam replied, "I guess that's proof that you never did read any of my journal. There isn't any sex in there at all. I use it for my dreams, aspirations, and lessons that I learn as I go through life. Sure there are entries **about** sex, but I could never bring myself to write the details. More like how I felt about it, and in one very special case how it had changed my life."

"I should have known," Philip said, mentally chastising himself. "I guess I have known for a while, I just didn't want to let go."

Sam looked slightly confused at this statement. "Let go of what?"

Smiling at her, and looking deep into her eyes Philip confessed. "Let go of you of course. From the moment we met I couldn't think of anything but you. I imagined how wonderful it would be to be with you, and I have to tell you that it certainly has lived up to everything I dreamed it would be. But I'm equally certain that you were meant for something bigger than me. You have a great spirit that needs one equally great. Something I'm not. I really wanted it to be me but now I realize that, with the greatest of intentions and effort, I wouldn't be equal to the life you are meant to live."

"Philip, I..." Sam began, but Philip quickly interrupted.

"No, there's no use trying to figure it out. I've been trying to figure it out as well but this is just one of those things I feel so deeply that I can't think myself out of it. Believe me I want to. Being with you makes me feel special. It makes me want to strive for something better than what I am, but in the end I know I can't. I'm sorry if you feel tricked at all. I'm not brushing you off or anything." Philip laughed nervously. "Far from it in fact. I guess you could say I feel so strongly about you I have to put your destiny before my needs. I really want to stay friends with you though. It's so hard to find anyone with your…um…quality is as close as I can get to describing it."

After stopping to inhale a long breath, Philip realized he had run through his entire speech without pausing. He waited both nervous and expectant, for Sam's response. She looked at him hard, as though trying to see right into his brain to discern his thoughts. Finally she seemed to come to a decision.

"I was going to argue that you don't really know me enough to say those things," Sam admitted. "But then I realized that you are sincere, and that you feel this right down to the bone. Any argument I could make might change your mind but wouldn't change your heart. I suppose I have to admit that I panicked a bit. Even though I don't know you that well either we did share something special." After a brief pause Sam smiled and added, "And I'd really like to get more of those excellent neck massages."

Philip couldn't help but laugh at the implied entendre, and truth be told he hoped it meant what he thought it did but he didn't want to push anything. "For a friend, any time."

The two of them smiled and embraced again. Sam knew that the evening was far from over (at least if she had anything to say about it). But for the moment she was content to lie there with him, basking in the warm afterglow.

Untamed Woman

"What do you think Philip, should I take this job or not?" Sam's question was sincere, attempting to remain objective so that she wouldn't unduly influence her friend's answer.

Philip looked at her askance, briefly wondering what was going through her mind. Over the months he had learned better than to question her motives though. Sam was one of those rare people with absolute integrity. She meant everything she said and there was never any hidden motive in her conversation.

In a way Philip felt honored that she had grown to trust him and his opinions so much that she asked about this particular issue that he knew was so dear to her. In the end there could only be one answer.

"Without a doubt. In fact you should start it as soon as you can – right now in fact." He hoped his own sincerity would shine through as much as hers. This was the big break she had been hoping and working for. He couldn't imagine her turning down this job. Not when she had gone so far in pursuit of her dream.

Rose in Bloom

"I agree. It's settled then. As of Monday morning the Museum of Antiquities will have a new researcher. Little do they realize that by this time next year they will have a field expert as well, willing to travel to far-off exotic locations to dig in the dirt and find cool stuff."

"And may God have mercy on them, trying to keep up with everything that you'll have to offer them."

Sam chuckled at the somewhat backhanded compliment. The easy confidence with which she and Philip now conversed made it easy to find and accept his true sentiment. "Thank you kind sir, I shall do my best to keep them on their toes."

"Make them wonder where you get all your energy is more like it," Philip continued. "Honestly Sam I can't see how you can do everything that you do and stay so lively and cheerful."

"The secret my dear Philip," said Sam, walking over to Philip and planting herself firmly on his lap, "is to love what you do and do what you love. I have both." With that she leaned down and planted a kiss first on his forehead, then on his lips. Soon they were entangled in a passionate embrace that usually ended with the two of them smiling at each other over a rumpled set of bed sheets.

This time however Philip broke away and, looking into Sam's eyes asked her, "Now Sam, what would your latest boyfriend think?"

"Oh pish-tosh, you are my only boyfriend. The rest of them are just temporary lovers. Fun playthings with no real substance to them who are only after one thing, which just so happens to be what I'm after as well."

"Dumped another one did you?" Philip responded, with a keen insight born of many similar experiences.

"Okay, you got me. You know me too well." Sam sat up and gazed off into the distance. Philip knew this was a sign that her attention was wandering off to faraway places and deep inner thoughts.

"Hello, don't phase on me here. I'm getting a little worried. A year ago you wouldn't have had anything to do with a man and now you're tossing them aside like they're used paperclips."

Slowly Sam's attention returned to what Philip was saying. He knew better than to expect an instant response. Part of Sam always saying what she meant was her taking the time to internalize her thoughts and figure out herself what she wanted to say.

"There's nothing really to worry about. At least nothing you haven't already heard a thousand times. I feel incomplete, like a book without a cover, a peach without a pit,…"

"Peanut butter without jelly?" joked Philip.

"Laugh if you want but yes, that's exactly what I mean. There's something bigger, outside myself that I'm not seeing and not experiencing. I don't know what it is but it's driving me crazy feeling that it's out there but I'm not being able to grab hold of it."

"Sounds like someone is pining for 'true love'," Philip added sagely. "Maybe you need to put aside sex for the moment and try to meet some men who stimulate you intellectually, emotionally, spiritually, whatever."

"You mean ugly boring men don't you?" giggled Sam. "Alright, not a fair comment. Maybe you're right, there must be someone out there that has that mysterious something I'm missing. When everything you try doesn't work it's time to try something new, no matter **how dumb it sounds**." Philip was undaunted by the emphasis on the last phrase. He was sure that she understood and agreed with him, she just wanted to point out that it wasn't her idea.

"In the meantime," she continued, "If I'm not getting any sex from the endless stream of meaningless relationships in my life whatever shall I do?"

Never one to miss such an obvious cue Philip was quick to reply, "I guess somebody will have to make the sacrifice. Somebody kind, loving, sort-of-intelligent-but-not-enough-for-you… somebody who's lap you might sit on occasionally and somebody easy to seduce."

Sam smiled, eager to continue from where they had left off. "I guess since I can't find such a person I'll have to settle for you." She replayed the kiss that had started their conversation and this time Philip put up no resistance. After all, gazing at Sam from across the bed sheets was one of his favorite pastimes.

Whisked Away

It was a full year that Sam had been working at the museum when she met him. Chad Barrington the third was one of the museum's patrons. He donated a lot of time and money to the search and preservation of antiquities. Sam had only noticed in passing that he was devastatingly handsome. (At least that's what she told herself.) He had the kind of looks that only a lifetime devoid of hard labor could provide. His features were chiseled but soft – well defined and unworn.

Though she had never met him, Sam had often fantasized about him. He would whisk her away to some Greek Isle and confess his mad passion for her, then make love to her from dusk to dawn in his magnificent villa overlooking the ocean while baby porpoises cavorted outside his bedroom.

At least I haven't lost my capacity to daydream, Sam mumbled to herself, suddenly aware that she had been leaning over an ancient text for several minutes without actually reading a single character.

Rose in Bloom

Just then the curator walked in to her office with Chad in tow. It wasn't unusual for the two of them to be together but usually it was touring the latest acquisitions. They had never come to see her research before. Even more unusual was the curator introducing the two of them since he usually insisted on keeping arm's length between patrons and the museum staff.

"Chad Barrington the third, meet Samantha Sinclair. Samantha, this is Chad, one of our..."

"Patrons," interrupted Sam, "Yes I've seen his name on many of the acquisition forms. It's a pleasure to meet you Mr. Barrington." Even though she was feeling a bit sheepish at meeting the man she had just been daydreaming about her strength shone through.

"A pleasure to meet you too Samantha," replied Chad. There was a hint of some kind of accent in his speech but Sam couldn't quite place it. It couldn't be Greek, could it?

"Please, call me Sam."

"Agreed Sam, if you also will call me Chad."

The curator interrupted with a slight air of impatience over the obvious flirting underway. "Samantha, Chad has a most interesting proposition for us which I thought might be of particular interest to you." Despite her insistence the curator refused to call her Sam, which she hated so much that she continued to think of and address him as 'the curator' with no particular name. It was a small piece of defiance, which no doubt annoyed him, but she couldn't make him understand what that name represented to her and why it was so important that she left it behind.

At present though her focus was elsewhere, her eyes never left Chad while he spoke. She replied to him directly, oblivious that the curator had said anything at all.

"How fascinating, what do you have in mind Chad?"

Chad began explaining his proposal to Sam. He spoke of a legendary text that had been lost for centuries. A team of his recently stumbled across it while performing some routine investigative digs. The text was said to contain 'great secrets of a grave and serious nature' but no details had ever been available. He was fascinating to listen to, this Chad. He spoke as a storyteller might, weaving fact and fiction together, providing interesting observations and his own coloring, keeping Sam enrapt for his entire explanation.

"That sounds immensely interesting Chad, but where is it that I come in? Surely your team can continue the investigation?"

"You would think so Sam," he replied, keeping his eyes firmly locked to hers, almost hypnotically. "The problem they ran into is that the text is in no known language. They suspect it is a regional dialect from a region that bordered two distinct areas. Two languages meshed together, plus a local dialect thrown in just to make it interesting."

"Like the French/English combinations spoken throughout various parts of Québec. All similar, all rooted in two languages, yet each distinctly different," Sam interrupted, completing his thought.

"Exactly. It seems there is more to you than a pretty smile." Sam winced at such a transparent compliment yet

Rose in Bloom

somehow it seemed sincere, causing her to blush ever so slightly. "Flattery is not necessary," she scolded, "I know my stuff."

"Apparently so, and it is for that exact reason your curator here has recommended I see you for this exacting assignment. We need a translation of these pages and the area where we hypothesize the origins to be just so happens to be your specialty."

This was too good to be true, thought Sam - this choice assignment dropping right into her lap, right in her area of expertise. She mentally shrugged at her good fortune and decided not to look a gift horse in the mouth. "I guess you know all about me then, and yet I know so little about you. What exactly is your offer?"

Chad smiled, seeming pleased at Sam's interest. "My offer for the moment is to invite you to dinner where I can both explain the assignment details and let you find out about me so that we are on an even footing." The gleam in his eye was unreadable, but Sam's recent fantasies filled in all sorts of details.

Fortunately, or unfortunately depending on how Sam chose to look at it, Chad was a perfect gentleman at dinner. He selected a fine restaurant with delicious food, elegant atmosphere and exquisite service. He talked freely about his background, jokingly referring to himself as a 'silver spoon child'.

His interest in antiquities arose from his parents' habit of collecting all manner of rare artifacts in their travels. They mostly bought them for investment and aesthetic value, but Chad saw something deeper. He was able to look at an item and project himself back into the time where it was created and used. Many a night were spent imagining what it was like being at the feet of the Pharaohs of Egypt, or attending court for Louis XIV. So deep was his fascination of other cultures from the past that he began mounting his own expeditions to dig for less valuable but more interesting artifacts.

In fact the book he was searching for was just such an artifact. As a physical piece it wasn't remarkable, yet it held the key to the union of two cultures. Neighboring states from this era were almost always at war with each other, or at least engaged in petty squabbling, yet somehow this particular area managed to establish a friendly, even synergetic trade relationship. The key seemed to be in the culture that arose from living at the border between the two states, and this book promised to divulge the secrets of how those people lived.

Chad went on to explain to Sam how he had earlier researched this book and kept hitting dead-end after dead-end in his quest, until finally he gave up. If it weren't for the fact that he had been supervising the particular dig that found this book it probably would have been tossed aside as irrelevant and unimportant. Now his prize was in hand and he was determined to do anything necessary to claim it.

Sam had sat fascinated by the tale that Chad wove. It was interesting already just by nature of the material, being her specialty, yet something about the way he spoke made it come alive for her. She could see his passion in his story, and understood immediately why he had spent his time studying and imagining with those artifacts regarded by his parents as mere financial investments.

Some caution still prevailed in her though, so she held back from her first instinct of leaping at the opportunity.

"Okay so now I know the history. If there is no other information on this culture how do you expect me to be able to decipher anything? The regional dialects alone are usually enough to obscure a single language, with two it will be all but unreadable gibberish."

That was what she said out loud, but it was more to check Chad's commitment and temper. In her mind she was already spinning dozens of scenarios for how she could unravel the secrets of this mystery text.

"I see by your expression that you are already thinking of ways to decipher this 'unreadable gibberish'," noted Chad. Damn, was she that transparent? Or had it been so long since something had sparked her interest like this that it was written all over her face.

"Not to underestimate your no doubt prodigious talent for solving this type of riddle, you will need more information than you can find in your books for this one. The area in question lost almost all of its written records in the great fire at the Library of Alexandria. Only this book remained untouched, which is why it is so valuable. Unfortunately it also means that without external references there is nothing to compare it to – no Rosetta Stone as it were. I do however have a solution to propose."

"Go on, I'm listening," she replied, in a casual manner. Her balloon was only deflated a little by Chad's new information. She figured that despite the problems she could still figure it out, but if he had a better idea it couldn't hurt to listen.

"My proposal is this – to take you out to the actual site where we believe the border between the two states existed. There are still people inhabiting the area, as well as a few abandoned ruins. Although they are many generations removed from the people I seek they may still contain some essential clues to finding the history."

Intellectually Sam grudgingly had to admit that it was a very solid approach to finding hidden information - kind of like returning to the scene of the crime to look for clues. Even though the "crime" in question happened millennia ago there still might be some useful clues. After all, the dinosaurs left clues that lasted millions of years.

Once the analytical side of her went quiet Sam felt a slight chill run down her spine as she realized where she was going. The people as Chad had described them through dinner could only have come from one place – Methana, a small island off the coast of Greece. Her daydream was coming true!

She quickly spoke to bring herself back to reality. "Okay Mister Chad Barrington Eye-Eye-Eye, you have engaged my services. You'll notice I didn't ask how much you are willing to pay since I'm assuming that you being willing to fly me to Greece means that you think I'm worth a lot. I'll rely on your integrity to match the payment of my services for the museum to my value." The confidence had returned to Sam as she looked at Chad, almost daring him to consider short-changing her.

"Excellent Sam, we'll leave tomorrow!"

"We? You mean you're going with me?"

"Of course, you can't expect me to just let you run wild all over the land without the benefit of my expertise and experience. You may have figured out that it's Greece you're bound for but I'm the one who has mapped out the ancient borders in exquisite detail and who knows exactly where to get the most useful information."

Rose in Bloom

"Since you're also the man paying the bills I guess it can't hurt to have you along, but I warn you, don't get in my way because I might bite when I'm cornered!"

Chad didn't answer, leaving Sam wondering if he were considering the possibly pleasant interpretations of her threat. He only smiled and handed her the already prepared plane ticket. He obviously had a lot of confidence in his ability to convince her to go. They quickly said their goodnights and arranged a time to meet at the airport the following day.

Grecian Sun

The plane gently touched down at the small airport. Sam tried not to look nervous as they landed, although never having flown before she wasn't quite sure what to expect from the flight. It had in fact been fairly smooth and uneventful but she still jumped at every slightly bump and creak of the plane.

The midday sun beat down on the tarmac, creating a hotplate for them to walk over from their plane. On the flight Chad had not talked with Sam much, being engrossed in his maps and topography charts. He apparently hadn't figured it out so precisely as he had intimated. Sam didn't mind, as it gave her time to study the book. Or rather study the computerized version of the book that he had scanned and brought along.

She hadn't thought about it in advance but with the accuracy in computer scanning these days it didn't make sense to risk the book itself on this trip. Of course having the actual book always made the information seem more real to Sam, like there was a connection to the author from days long past. This would have to do though, and it did afford her some better tools to help in the translation as she pored over it.

After several fruitless hours the book started to look pretty impervious to her understanding. Words and symbols here and there looked familiar but they were arranged in odd ways, in some cases not even right side up. It was like trying to read and understand a bowl of alphabet soup.

She was glad the plane had landed to give her a chance to clear her head.

They got underway relatively quickly. Chad had hired the local equivalent of a limousine to take them to their destination. Sam had half-expected this destination to be isolated, in the middle of nowhere. When the driver came to a stop and Chad announced that they had arrived she saw not open countryside but a bustling metropolis. They were in the middle of a city.

"You can't be serious," she challenged. "You expect me to poke around here in a city?"

"Sam, you surprise me. Surely you realize that the passage of time doesn't always cover ancient civilizations in sand and sea."

Blushing slightly Sam mentally chastised herself. Of course she realized that, she just formed assumptions in her mind and let them guide her thinking. "Sorry, bad move on my part. It won't happen again."

Because she hadn't attempted to explain or blame anything on her relatively small slip Sam had gone up in Chad's estimation. Anyone who is right all the time can be confident and self-assured, but it took a special person to make mistakes and still retain their faith in themselves.

"Let me show you the dig," Chad continued. "It started out as a construction project but once they had gone down a few meters I realized what lay below and immediately canceled the development so that a proper dig could be mounted."

Sure enough Chad's "dig" was a large lot between two tall buildings. It was dwarfed on either side, necessitating special stadium lighting to overcome the shadows of the city. Chad led the way down the spiral ramp to the bottom of the dig.

"This," he proclaimed proudly, "is where the book was recovered. It was found sealed inside an urn, which was the only reason it was so well preserved. We've been scouring this area looking for other artifacts but we haven't found a thing. Our current working theory is that the book was placed in the urn and buried deep so that its wisdom would be preserved. Either that or so that its evil was out of reach," Chad added, grinning slyly at Sam.

"Evil urn, preserved forever, gotcha," said Sam, completely distracted by the layers and layers of the dig surrounding her. To think that centuries ago this was the center of a thriving civilization who had escaped the ravages of war in an era where nobody was left untouched.

"Oh you're off thinking again, aren't you?" Chad noticed. "I know how that is. Being here often has the same effect on me. It's as if I can reach back…"

"…and hear the voices of the people," interrupted Sam. "Now if only those people would tell us their secrets our job would be much easier." Sam's little joke broke the

Rose in Bloom

moment of reverie and she caught Chad looking intently at her.

"Sam, it's been a long flight. I thought it important to show you the dig as soon as possible but both of us could use a little dinner and some rest, don't you agree?"

It was hard to argue with that logic. As soon as it was said out loud Sam noticed that her body had become weary on the trip. A little food and maybe a hot bath might be just the thing she needed. "You're right, that sounds good. Does this place we're staying at have hot water?"

Chad laughed, knowing exactly what she was asking. "Yes Sam, although it's sometimes hard to come by I always insist on having a plentiful supply of hot water wherever I go. Something about soaking in a hot tub is so … therapeutic, that I wouldn't dream of depriving myself."

As they began driving away from the dig Sam noticed that in all directions the city slowly faded away down to nothing. It was as though she was standing at the center of creation and things had built up around her. Even by Western definitions this was clearly an affluent area, yet when studying the region she had not thought it would be. It had no central waterway, no easy access through or around harsh terrain, and was not a logical stopping point for weary travelers. In short this area had no reason for existing in the way it did. By all rights it should have been exactly as Sam had first imagined it – a lonely countryside with barren land and a few small roads leading to the real centers of the ancient world. She thought it odd but it was quickly forgotten as they headed out towards their destination.

The villa looked like something out of a fairy tale. The walls were stone, yet possessed a brilliant pale color that was nothing like the plain sand coloring of the common resident. The red terracotta roof was clearly imported and out of place here, yet provided a nice contrast to the basic construction materials. The wrought iron gates swung open to reveal a small garden inside. Most of the flowers Sam did not recognize, and they all were remarkable in their own way – brilliant petals on one, exotic shaping on another. The drive swung around the red pebble driveway, circling the tiered fountain that resided in the center.

"Well it's not much but it does provide the comforts of home," Chad casually remarked.

For a long moment Sam's mouth hung open wondering exactly what the comforts of home looked like if he considered this lavish estate "not much".

"I hope you don't mind staying here in my villa Sam. I've found even the best hotels in this area lack the simple amenities I've grown accustomed to."

His villa, Sam thought. That explains a lot. She idly wondered how many of these villas or equivalents Chad actually possessed or had access to. It was painfully evident exactly why Chad was able to provide funding for the museum and many of its endeavors. Next to maintenance on places like this the money he provided would seem like pocket change to him.

"Come, let me show you to the master bathroom. Water access is at a premium here so much as I would have liked to have a bath in every bedroom I was only able to convince the local authorities to allow me the one and increase my water allowance. There was some nonsense about overtaxing their meager desalinization capabilities. I didn't follow everything they were saying but the local laws have very strict rules on what water usage you're allowed. They have plenty of water to drink of course but for some reason don't provide for bathing. I could use ocean water I suppose but it's just not the same."

Most of the long explanation was lost on Sam. She was simply following along to the bath and was too tired at the moment to care much about the local customs, water usage, and other details. Right now there was a hot bath with her name on it and she intended to claim it.

The bathroom itself was huge and ornate. Marble covered the floor and most of the fixtures including the bathtub. It was quite a sizable one too, set into the corner with a large gold-trimmed mirror on the walls surrounding it and had already been filled with steaming water. Chad must have called ahead and instructed the household staff to start it for him. She felt a little bit special that he was allowing her to go first.

Chad left the room with a promise to return in an hour after she had time to properly relax. Sam looked at herself in the large ornate mirror over the bathtub. She looked as tired as she felt. Her hair hung limply over her shoulders and her eyelids sagged as though desperately trying to close themselves and bring sleep to Sam.

Slowly she slipped her shirt up over her head and slid her pants off. Although it was the fatigue that prevented her from moving very quickly there was a sensuality in the motion that brought the hint of a smile to her face. Looking up into the mirror again she saw a little bit more life in her. Her arms crossed over, and reaching her hands up to her shoulders she squeezed softly. There was only a small bit of tension there, but it sure felt good to relieve it. The relaxation spread down into her arm and one hand slid down off her shoulder over her breast. Her eyes closed involuntarily as she stroked the top and then slipped her fingertips behind the thin fabric onto her nipple. A shiver went down her spine as she squeezed it between her fingers.

"…thought you might like this…," came the voice as someone barged in through the door. "Oops, pardon me, I thought you weren't getting ready just yet." It was Chad who had sent Sam scrambling to first remove her hand from her bra and second to grab a towel to cover up anything else he might be seeing.

Chad had turned to face the door until Sam was covered again. "Don't you knock?" she said, only slightly annoyed at the intrusion.

"I did knock, and there was no answer so I thought it safe to come in." At least Chad was being a gentleman, choosing to omit any specifics of what he might have seen when he entered. And what **had** he seen anyway, Sam wondered.

"Well now that you've interrupted my undressing you can at least tell me the reason for your barging in," snapped Sam.

"Certainly. I just thought you might like this particular bath oil. It's made from the pressings of Egyptian cotton combined with some of the most fragrant plants on this side of the world. It has a heavenly aroma and will leave your skin feeling silky smooth."

"You sound like a commercial," Sam said gruffly, still undecided if she should be happy about his arrival. A small voice in the back of her head whispered a tiny hope that he had seen her and was turned on by what he saw, but she quickly silenced it. "Okay I'll take your bath oil if you promise not to barge in any more!"

"It's a deal," returned Chad, sounding as though she were doing him a favor by accepting his generosity. "As advance warning of my next arrival it will be in exactly one hour, judged by that clock on the wall across from you."

Sam looked up. She hadn't noticed a clock before but that was only because it melded so well with the décor. Noting the time she nodded and then shooed him away so that she could return to her bath before the water cooled.

The door closed behind Chad and Sam released the breath she had been half-holding since his arrival. It was exciting in a way to be standing in front of him so vulnerable, only a towel covering her - far better than her daydream in fact. And despite the obvious opportunity he had behaved like a perfect gentleman. Not once did she catch him trying to peek around for an area she might have inadvertently left uncovered. That was as it should be… wasn't it?

After removing her lingerie Sam stepped gingerly into the tub. It was still quite hot, but not quite so hot that it was uncomfortable. Clearly the staff knew what they were doing. The candles around the tub were a nice touch too, she thought. All I need now is the lights down and some music on.

After sliding below the water until she was submerged up to her neck Sam looked around the tub and saw something she had overlooked before. After marveling for a second on the superb design that went into this bathroom to keep things so subtle and hidden she sat up to investigate. It was a control panel of some sort with several buttons on it.

Logically pressing any of these buttons should be perfectly safe, thought Sam, calming her brief entertainment of the remote possibility of her comforting soak being interrupted with an abrupt electrical surge. They weren't laid out in any logical sequence, or labeled in any way. Might as well try the first one first, Sam reasoned, boldly striking the leftmost button.

The reaction was immediate but subtle. The lights throughout the room dimmed slowly, stopping just short of full darkness. The positioning of the lights really gave the impression of candlelight.

"Oho, so it's a mind-reading device," Sam said out loud, to nobody in particular. "Let's see what's behind button number 2!" Out leapt her finger to the second button. She felt a slight tingling sensation beneath her. It grew slightly stronger but the bubbles breaking the surface revealed the Jacuzzi jets from which the tingling originated.

Very impressive, thought Sam. Other than the faint pop…pop…pop… of the bubbles releasing at water level the jets was completely silent. Sam had visited the hot tub at the school gym several times but always thought the roar of the jets below her ruined the relaxation of the experience. Clearly this was a problem that could be solved with a judicious application of time, expertise and, of course, money.

Two buttons remained untried, but the positive reinforcement of the previous two made Sam not a bit shy about reaching to try them out. The third brought

Rose in Bloom

the soft strains of classical music from speakers that were apparently built right into the walls themselves. The white marble was not as solid as it appeared yet despite an earnest effort by Sam to locate the source of the music the wall failed to yield its secrets.

Reaching for the final button Sam muttered half to herself, "C'mon chilled champagne and strawberries!" forcing a laugh at the ridiculousness of her request, yet not quite convinced that it wasn't precisely what would arise.

"Yes madam, how may I be of service?"

Sam jumped, startled by the sudden new voice behind her yet not so unaware of her unclothed condition that she rose up to find out what was going on. "Service? I mean… what do you mean, be of service?"

She kept her back to the stolid upright man behind her. Her brief glance showed that he must have been some sort of servant, dressed impeccably in a fine black suit with white gloves. "You rang for service, madam, and I am here to provide it. What might I do for you?"

"Ummm…", stammered Sam, not used to this kind of attention and unsure of how to respond. Quickly she regained enough composure to resurrect her last thought, "You wouldn't happen to have champagne and strawberries would you?"

"Very good madam." The man disappeared silently through the door and reappeared moments later with a small silver bucket with a bottle of champagne and a silver tray with freshly washed strawberries invitingly arranged. "Will there be anything else madam?"

"No, thank you. I mean, if there is I know how to reach you right?"

Taking that as dismissal the man left Sam alone once more. She stared unbelievingly at the strawberries and champagne (no doubt a fine vintage but she wouldn't have known the difference) before digging in. Now this, she thought as her teeth sunk into the soft, yielding flesh of the strawberry, is something I could get used to.

Laying back in the tub and shipping her champagne Sam soon found her mind drifting about in all directions. She closed her eyes and thoughts of her adventure appeared in front of her, dressed up in fanciful garb. No longer was this a strictly-business trip to satisfy academic curiosity and discover the past; now it was a fanciful journey through a fairytale land of pink unicorns and handsome knights with their castles full of servants waiting on her every whim. Reality dissolved for Sam as the relaxation reached right down to her core and even the mental tension that seemed to pervade her thoughts was erased.

As Sam's mind drifted she imagined herself frolicking in the ocean with a school of dolphins. They would sing to her in their dolphin way and she, with her newly sprouted mermaid tail, would swim alongside them and sing with them. Their music was soft and, for lack of a better word, spiritual. It spoke to Sam at a deep level and she couldn't help but respond to them.

As she swam about with them singing, she noticed a handsome young prince leaning over the edge of a ship, looking down on them. He seemed fascinated by their song, and watched enrapt as they playfully chased alongside his ship. Sam-the-mermaid was curious about this prince, and increased her song, directing it towards him even though she knew he wouldn't understand.

Rose in Bloom

He continued to watch her and even tried to join her song. But he was no dolphin and the discordance of his human voice blended poorly with the lilting melody of the dolphins. Soon the dolphins departed, no doubt in search of an area where they could let their song ring out uninterrupted but Sam-the-mermaid stayed with the man. She listened as his song grew louder in her ears. It was not dolphin-song but it was strangely attractive. Louder and louder it grew, until it seemed to occupy her whole world, echoing like thunder and drowning out her own song.

Sam opened her eyes and without thinking shouted out, "Quiet, noisy human." She turned a deep crimson when she realized that she was no longer dreaming, but was now wide-awake and in the bathroom she entered what seemed like a lifetime earlier. Sitting in front of her was Chad, wearing an indiscernible smile.

"I've had many comments on my singing before, but I have to admit this is the first time anyone has called me a 'noisy human'."

"Oh Chad, I'm so sorry," Sam quickly apologized. "I wasn't talking to you, I was dreaming about dolphins and mermaids and a prince looking down into the water at me."

There was a brief pause as Sam's eyes slitted with a sudden realization of her situation. "Wait a minute, what are you doing here anyway? Come to see a naked lady? Did your butler 'Igor' tip you off, and you had to see for yourself? Real and spectacular, was that what he said?" Sam felt flushed from the sudden switch from defense to offense. She was not about to let him have the satisfaction of intimidating her at this point, so despite the fact that she knew her breasts were exposed above the waterline in the tub she held his eyes locked, almost daring him to look down.

Chad looked unfazed, returning her stare with an intensity so deep that it appeared effortless. "No actually, and his name is James, not 'Igor', although he would be quite amused at the reference." Sam watched him carefully but he didn't quaver for an instant.

"What you've failed to realize in your relaxed dream world is that the hour at which I promised to appear has arrived. I've learned that there's nothing as important as keeping my word and the fact that you were still unclothed (as-it-were) is certainly not going to deter me."

Sam felt slightly embarrassed, not because of her nudity, but because she had been so quick to leap to the wrong conclusion about Chad's motives.

Once again Chad showed himself to be extremely perceptive by remarking, "Oh don't be embarrassed, any male in my situation would have exactly those motives. In fact to tell the truth I'm finding it exceedingly difficult to keep my concentration at the moment so I would be obliged if you'd cover yourself up in some way so that we can get our dinner."

Sam realized that their eyes were still locked together and felt that this was a rare opportunity for her to have the upper hand in their dealings so she decided to press her advantage a little.

"So I'm making it difficult to concentrate am I?" she teased. "Well it wasn't my decision to have you barge in here while I was enjoying a rather perfect moment of relaxation," she continued, slowly rising from the water, "so I think you will have to just put a little extra effort into keeping your mind…" She paused for effect as one foot stepped out of the tub. "…on…" the second foot stepped out. "…business," she finished, stretching lazily upward and reaching back to wring the water out of the lower part of her hair.

Although Chad's eyes had not left hers she could see the longing grow in them. She had succeeded in breaking his 'legendary' concentration, and was slow to reach for a towel and give him some relief.

He had not moved, no doubt afraid to reveal the effect she had had on him. As she brushed past him to fetch her clothes she leaned over and whispered into his ear. "It's too bad you were too busy maintaining your concentration to enjoy what I had to offer. Maybe next time." Slinking out of the room her heart thumped loudly in her chest. There was no subtlety to that last comment, she might was well have jumped on him without the towel and begged him to have his way right there. The excitement she felt was both from fear and anticipation, knowing that it may have been a huge mistake, but she had placed the ball in his court now.

She didn't see him again when she returned to the bathroom to brush her hair out before going down to dinner. There must be some secret entrance there that is hidden as cleverly as the speakers in the wall were. It was just as well – she wasn't quite sure she wanted their next encounter to be in such an intimate setting after what she had said.

A few quick strokes of the brush later she was ready and fairly skipped down to the dinner table. It was surprisingly small and cozy. She half-expected a big long 'Citizen Kane' type table with her on one end and him a phone-call away on the other end. It was just a small hand-carved dining room table, probably seating only 6 at the most if there was a middle leaf that could be added.

The room was dimly lit, highlighted by two tall tapers on the table itself, set in simple silver bases. The serving set was china, of course, with nickel-brass silverware and two lead-crystal goblets apiece, presumably for both water and wine. Not surprisingly the meal was brought out in several courses, starting with soup, then salad.

So far Chad had not said anything to Sam, so she decided to break the silence, wondering if it was caused by her earlier forwardness. "Quite an elaborate meal for something whipped together just for us." It was an open-ended comment, which she hoped would give him a reason to talk with her while avoiding any discomfort he might be feeling. Of course she failed to consider that he was after all a man, and as such was not really so susceptible to embarrassment when beautiful women made their intentions known.

"To tell you the truth," he began, "I had planned for something a little more intimate, but then I thought that you might interpret it as another come-on, so I told the staff to serve 'the usual'." What he didn't mention was the rest of that instruction, 'the usual dinner for a dignitary or royalty'. He knew that might not go over well with the fiercely independent Sam.

"I'm glad that you were able to change your plans without too much trouble, but you didn't have to do that for me. I like small and intimate, and I don't recall ever saying that I didn't like come-ons... when they're welcome of course."

It didn't take much imagination on Chad's part to realize that for whatever reason Sam now wanted him for purposes that were definitely not businesslike. He smiled, now knowing how the evening would end, and happy that he had someone who understood the fine art of teasing and foreplay. "In that case I have a confession to make. I took advantage of a brief weakness in your gaze earlier to see that which I wasn't supposed to see."

Sam dropped her fork in mock horror. "I'm positively shocked." With a slight pause, coyly gazing downward she lowered her voice and added, "that you would think you weren't supposed to see it." Her voice rose back up, along with one eyebrow, "Weakness in my gaze?" she added incredulously.

"Yes, but only slight. You see, whenever people are thinking about something in the past – remembering - their gaze shifts to the side. When you were recalling your dream yours did exactly that and I could not resist. Most humble apologies, it won't happen again."

"Not to worry, you will never see my naked body **by accident** in the future." Sam was enjoying this subtle wordplay. It gave her a chance to let her inner child out to play but on an adult level. She wondered exactly how it would be that this man would find himself in her bed tonight, but she was certain that one way or another it would happen.

"Accidents have a habit of being accidental. I'm sure you couldn't prevent such a thing unless one of two things should occur. Either you would have to never be naked again while I was in the same general area, something which would make your stay here eventually quite... uncomfortable... or, you would have to wander around naked all of the time such that every time I saw your naked body it was no accident at all."

"I'll have to consider which of those two options affords me the most opportunity for enjoying my visit. Certainly the latter just won't do while I'm working, even though it does have its attraction."

Being no stranger to the language of the face Sam knew that Chad's eyes flitting upwards meant that he was visualizing exactly that. She wondered if he pictured her wearing only a tool belt and sandals, or completely unadorned. "Yes I should think I would cause quite a stir there, especially since most of the workers are undersexed men. I would most probably need your assistance to protect my honor."

"I would be honored to protect you," retorted Chad, and it was Sam's turn to picture Chad pouncing between her and her many new admirers eager to take a closer look or chance a touch here or there.

In truth these thoughts were turning Sam on more than a little. It was with somewhat of a relief that the final course was cleared, although there was a feeling of incompleteness that she couldn't quite put her finger on.

"Dessert, if you're wondering, is not quite chilled yet and will be served later. I can offer you a coffee or tea now but as for myself I always find that it just doesn't bring the same finality to the meal if it's out of order. A little compulsive I admit but some habits of civilization do have their purposes."

Sam declined for the moment, knowing that either of the drinks would take away part of that relaxed feeling she had achieved in the bath. Her immediate attention was on continuing her flirting with Chad in such a way

Rose in Bloom

that he knew exactly what was on her mind. She had grown to love speaking her thoughts straight-out but that would have spoiled the game they were playing. That's the trouble with subtlety, she sighed. You never know if you were fully understood.

"So you're waiting for things to chill off before proceeding are you?" It wasn't a particular inspired thought but the silence had begun to grow and Sam feared that Chad would suddenly lose interest before her desires were known.

"Indeed. Sometimes I find leaving things to chill is precisely the way to make the actual experience much sweeter when they finally do arrive."

"So long as the chilling process doesn't make them unpalatable."

"And so long as in being chilled they don't lose sight of how much they are desired."

There wasn't much doubt about what he was talking about now. Clearly her message had gotten through to him and he was completely agreeable. Suddenly the wait seemed unimportant and Sam decided to nudge things along a bit.

"Desirability is always there, and sometimes they want to be tasted as much as you want to eat them." A small tinge appeared behind Sam's ear. Only the most naïve of people could interpret this particular comment in an innocent way.

Chad seemed nonplussed, continuing to return her increasingly provocative banter. "But still the chill is necessary, so that when I run my tongue around the edge it doesn't melt prematurely. I like a dessert that lasts a long time so that I can enjoy every bit of it."

That was it, Sam's patience for subtlety had been bested and she could take no more. "Would you like to come up to my room and have dessert served there instead?"

Without answering, Chad rose to his feet and offered her his hand. Sam stood up, leaning slightly on him. The two of them turned towards the stairway, pausing slightly at the kitchen door for Chad to poke his head in and change his instructions.

Sam felt like she had returned to the fairy-tale. Here she was in this castle-like villa, arm-in-arm with a handsome prince, being swept off her feet and taken upstairs. Her footing was shaky, as her legs had begun to tremble slightly, but she continued on elegantly, as the heroine in a fairy-tale would have.

The door swung open and the two of them entered. As the door closed behind Chad he barely had time to latch it before feeling Sam's lips reach up against his. She could feel instantly that he was as excited from their dinner conversation as she was, and reached down to show that she meant what she had been implying all night. Her hand stroked the outside of his pants, feeling him beneath the thin fabric. She felt him responding, his hand sliding down her front, returning that trembling sensation to her legs.

She couldn't help but moan softly as his hand skimmed past her navel between her legs. She knew he would be greeted by the moist proof of her excitement. He wasted no time in experiencing that moistness, slipping his hand lower to get beneath the hem of her dress, then rising back up to discover she only sported a thin pair of panties underneath.

Rose in Bloom

One finger disappeared inside her, then two, as she eagerly urged Chad inside. Her hand had been busy at work freeing him from his pants, which now lay at his feet. She gripped him firmly, slowly squeezing higher and lower, knowing that neither of them would last very long at this rate. In truth they had already been making love for hours, they were just now getting to the sex part.

On that thought she dropped to her knees, letting Chad's hand glide upwards against her, taking her dress with it. He hesitated slightly, trying to keep his hand in contact with the breast that he had so coyly sneaked a peek of earlier. But Sam had a different target in mind for now, so he had to be content with a brief squeeze as she continued downward.

Her dress was half off, covering her head. She didn't finish the disrobing for the moment, content to hide in her colorful little world. It took a little tugging to remove Chad's underwear owing to his current state, but soon she had done just that. Her mouth then found its target, sliding as far onto it as she could. He tasted sweet, obviously not having missed his own bath when spying on hers. His hands found the side of her head, stroking her hair through the dress that still hung there. One hand slid it aside and tossed it off. Looking up she saw his eyes closed as he leaned back, enjoying her touch.

She wasn't about to be satisfied with that though. It wasn't quite clear to her at the moment that he hadn't just completely seduced her for his own amusement, but the fact remained that she was here and wanted him. If he was only interested in seducing her he was clearly very good at it, but that didn't mean she couldn't get what she wanted as well. Come to think of it, maybe it was she who had seduced him. Who had made the first move anyway?

What the heck was she worrying about that for? No matter how they had arrived at this point it was clear what she wanted and what she needed to do to get it. Standing up slowly she pulled Chad toward the bed. The down-filled duvet still lay over top of it, not yet pulled back for the night. The maid was obviously waiting for the 'dessert' to be finished. Cynically Sam wondered how many women had been brought into this world and lured to Chad this way.

But no, banish those thoughts, none of that matters at the moment. Just as they reached the bed Sam turned and pushed Chad so that he tumbled helplessly back onto it. Quickly stripping her panties off she sat up and let him feel her wetness firsthand. It had indeed been a long time since her last close encounter with a man but the joyous sensation quickly refreshed her memory on why she enjoyed this so much.

It was hard to believe that in such a short time she had gone from admiring this untouchable man from afar to the position she now occupied astride him.

...

They had barely arranged the disheveled sheets and straightened out their hair when a discreet knock came at the door. "Dessert madam?" came the immediately recognizable voice from the other side.

"Certainly James, come right in," Sam responded in a regal manner. She was certainly not going to suggest anything in her tone of voice. The manservant entered the room silently, making Sam wonder just how his feet touched the ground. He dropped what looked like a slice of cheesecake onto the night table and, noticing Chad sitting alongside Sam, quietly but forcefully said "The master will take his dessert in here Emma," whereupon a matronly woman of about 50 entered with a similar plate containing an absolutely decadent looking slice of chocolate cake, dripping with chocolate syrup.

Noticing her glance Chad remarked, "Chocolate – it's my only weakness I'm afraid. It's forced me to swim many a lap that I would rather have avoided." They both chuckled at the little joke.

"I do believe I can help you in that area," remarked Sam as she playfully stole a forkful from his plate.

"Oh so now that you've had your way with me you think that entitles you to 'Grand Theft Chocolate' do you?" With that he scooped a forkful from Sam's plate and stuffed a second one from his own plate into his mouth before whisking the plate aside and shielding it from her.

"Go ahead and have your chocolate you big baby. You know what they say about it don't you?"

"I know a lot of things they say about it," returned Chad, not willing to concede the advantage to Sam just yet, "To which of them are you referring?"

"That the only reason people have sex is to provide some variety from chocolate," snickered Sam.

"Hmmm, you make a good point," countered Chad, "But I have another."

Leaning forward to listen to what Chad had to say Sam found herself suddenly on the floor, flattened by a surprise tackle. "Violence, tsk tsk. The last resort of the incompetent," she teased.

"Incompetent you say? Well we'll just have to see if round two doesn't change your mind about that."

Realization

The sun rose, peeking through the sheer drapes that adorned the window across from Sam's bed. Her eyes squinted momentarily as they adjusted to the newfound brightness. The other side of the pillows was unoccupied – Chad must have woken up earlier and snuck out without waking her.

Recalling the late night they had both enjoyed Sam couldn't help but smile - but there was something else in there too, something sad. It had to do with her daydream in the tub, but what was it?

As if on cue James entered into the room, silently as always, with a tray loaded with breakfast. "The master thought you might enjoy a breakfast in bed this morning before you head out to the dig."

"The master thought correctly," Sam replied, somewhat distracted by that nagging sensation at the back of her mind. "And apparently the master knows just what I like for breakfast too. Is there anything he doesn't know?"

"The master likes guests to feel welcome and at home. It is our job to make sure that happens Miss Sinclair, and as you can see, we do it very well."

"Most of the time, but I guess 'the master' neglected to mention how much I hate being called Miss Sinclair. You can call me Sam, I insist. In fact, if I catch you calling me anything else I'll tell the master that I saw you dancing a jig in the hallways."

"Very amusing Mi… Sam. Please let me know if there is anything else I can do for you." James turned to leave, but just as the door closed Sam could swear she saw him breaking out into a jig. It appears the servants do indeed take their duties very seriously, and have a sense of humor about it too.

That was it – the sense of humor. That's what was missing – from her dream, from Chad, from everything she had been doing here. Sam knew there was something that was not quite perfect about Chad, but on the surface everything seemed just so. His good looks, his good manners, and his wealth didn't hurt any either, but his sense of humor was very dry and biting. In fact it mostly seemed like even when he was joking he was very serious about it, like it was planned.

That's what the dream was trying to tell her. The cacophonic voice was just its way of saying that although he was very attractive in every way she could think of he didn't have that fire in the belly that drives all passionate men. Sam couldn't help but chuckle to herself, thinking of Chad as anything but passionate after last night, but this was different. It wasn't passion as in lust; it was passion as in a deep impenetrable devotion to something higher

Rose in Bloom

than him (for which this trinket expedition certainly didn't apply).

Or maybe he did have it, and just chose not to show it to her. It was all very confusing but Sam's inner voice was sending one message to her very clearly – have all of the fun you want with him, but he's not the one you're looking for.

As she absent-mindedly munched on a slice of whole-wheat toast Chad entered the room, having obviously been up for hours and now ready for the day. "Good morning lazy-bones, I hope you're enjoying the breakfast. I'm all ready to put you to work, slave-driver that I am."

Now that she had thought about it, it stood out like a beacon. He was joking, but it was forced. It was coming from a lifetime of knowing what people wanted to hear and feel, and giving it to them. He may not even realize that it was phony, but like the smile on an actor's face it was easy to recognize for what it was.

Oddly enough with this realization Sam felt no sense of loss. She would have expected that, like the first time you realize your parents don't know everything like you thought they did (not to be confused with the teenage years where they know absolutely nothing). But it wasn't there. Clearly they hadn't connected in that special way Sam had been looking for. At that moment she knew for certain there was no real future for them.

"Slave-driver…hmmm… that sounds interesting. You'll have to explain more of that to me tonight." Just because he wasn't "Mr. Right" didn't mean he couldn't be "Mr. Right Now" Sam thought. It was now obvious to her that he didn't feel that deeply for her either, so staying at this playful level while working together seemed to be a perfectly acceptable and comfortable compromise to her. Of course when she returned home she would have to resume her search for that magical connection that she felt even more convinced than ever must exist out there somewhere.

Once the work on the project began Sam found herself more and more fascinated by it. There was so much more to be found out here in the ancient dirt than could ever exist in the dust on the textbooks. Although she spent pretty much every evening with Chad she came to view him as little more than a pleasant diversion as the project devoured all of her attention.

To Chad everything had pretty much gone as planned. He had seduced the lovely intelligent woman, convinced her to spend the days finishing his project and her nights giving him her body. He knew that once she had uncovered the secrets of the book there would be a parting, and in the back of his mind he was vaguely concerned over the devastating effect it might have on Sam. But he had seen it before as the women came and went through his life so there was nothing particularly new in all this for him.

It was only a few weeks before Sam had unraveled the mystery the book had presented. At first she had very little luck as none of the nearby indigenous peoples recognized any of the scrawling in the book, but a key discovery at the dig site accelerated the investigation. A burial ground was uncovered showing some of the people from roughly the same time as the book, giving great clues into the society of the time.

One of the biggest clues was a man buried with arms crossed in the Egyptian style, wearing what looked like

Rose in Bloom

might have been some sort of ceremonial headdress, clutching a writing instrument in both hands. Beside him were a few scraps of papyrus in the same writing as the book, apparently describing his last Will and Testament, *including the objects to be buried with him.*

Armed with this crucial information Sam was able to put meaning to large sections of the text, but there was some odd repetition that couldn't be explained. It was by chance that a worker had brought in a shaving mirror one day because he was running so late. He apologized profusely about the delay, but after glimpsing a page she happened to be holding in his mirror Sam wrapped her arms around him and planted a big kiss on his unshaven face.

She snatched the mirror from his hand and ran to the trailer where the book and rest of the pages sat. The worker was sure he was in trouble at that point but not sure for what. In fact nothing could be further from the truth. He had provided Sam with a crucial key to deciphering the remainder of the text.

Holding them up to the mirror one at a time she shouted out loud "YES!!! THAT'S IT!!!" Chad burst through the door, demanding in his usual half-joking tone, "What's it? What's going on in here? And why aren't I doing it?"

"These pages," Sam began excitedly, "these pages are actually each several pages combined. The problem is that we've been assuming a uniform direction of writing, left-to-right, top-to-bottom, and trying to decipher them that way. When actually, thanks to my unshorn friend out there, I've just discovered that the writing goes in all different directions. That's why there's so much repetition!

That's why the body we dug up is clutching writing instruments in **both** hands. He was ambidextrous, and wrote in whatever way was most convenient."

"Well sure, and all that it implies," said Chad, not quite sure where Sam was headed with this.

"And why would anyone choose to write in such a way? There has to be a reason. Da Vinci wrote in backwards mirror script because he wanted to mask his secrets from others, and because he was a repressed left-hander who didn't want to conform to the right-handed writing style. I used printing for years because my writing was illegible. Doctors write in scrawling Latin on prescriptions to avoid panicking the patient. Don't you see? This man wrote this way because that's how he thought!" Sam was on a roll and ideas were just flying out of her mouth without stopping to ask directions. Chad sat listening, getting more and more confused by the second.

"So you have this people, poised between two states who want to tear each other apart. If they do that then what happens here? Think the 'No-Man's Land' of World War I – total destruction as the two enemies try to get to each other. What's the logical solution for this then? They can't leave their home, they can't get caught in the war around them, so they..." Sam paused, wondering if Chad would be able to fill in the blank.

"They..." he wasn't biting, and was still quite lost.

"They become peacekeepers. They mediate the fight between their two neighbors. They learn to listen to both sides of an argument at the same time, and to present it to the opposite side in a way that avoids hostility. But they can't write in a way that either side can read because they'll figure out what's going on and start a war just out of spite. So they mask their writing, and use both hands to capture both sides at once. I bet if I mirror this script it will match a lot of things written here and on other pages."

Sam felt like a dam had burst. A sudden energy filled her with the goal of getting to the bottom of the writing, and now at long last she had a direction to pursue. She scribbled furiously, copying down the mirror script into her computer using her writing stylus, then reversed sections, turned them on end, in short did everything she could think of to make them look like the words in other places.

It was only a matter of hours before she emerged from the trailer, several straightened pages in hand, and started walking to the nearest village. Instead of trying to find people that understood the whole thing now she just concentrated on finding the meaning of individual words. Not surprisingly a lot of them had been bastardized or fallen into disuse but there seemed to be someone everywhere who could manage to help out on a word here and there, now that they had been straightened out.

Sam marveled at the human being's evolved pattern-matching capabilities and how it actually hindered everyone from being able to recognize words simply because their direction had been changed. Once she had gathered all of the information she asked Chad to give her the computer and some peace and quiet so that she could collate her information and complete the arduous task of deciphering the semantics. Chad was a little put-out that all of a sudden Sam's energy had been diverted from him at night, but he had to yield in the face of such an onslaught of energy. The fact that the second night when he had managed to talk her into his bed she had sat bolt upright midway through the act and jumped out to enter something into her computer was the final straw. He left her alone for the time she needed, waiting for her to put this complex jigsaw together now that she had finally collected all of the pieces.

It was exactly 4 days 7 hours and 25 minutes later that she emerged from her room, looking a little bedraggled but smiling triumphantly. Chad knew the figure since he had written the exact time of her sequestering down in frustration earlier.

"I have it," she exclaimed, waving a handful of papers in the air. "I now know the secret. But I warn you, you may not like what I have to say."

"Sam after over 4 days of waiting, and a lifetime before that, I'm prepared for any answer you have to give me. What is it?"

He sounded confident but Sam detected a slight wince as she began. "This book is, for lack of better words, a recipe for peace. It describes in detail how to go about getting two hostile parties to sit down and negotiate with each other, even when each has nothing to gain from it. Even back then it must have had immense value, which probably explains the affluence in this region. These people must have been master traders. If they knew how to get hostile parties to agree then setting up trade negotiations and sales treaties must have been child's play to them."

"That's what it is, a recipe for peace? No secret treasure, no ancient secrets for immortality? Just peace?"

Rose in Bloom

"Really Chad, don't underestimate the value of peace. After all in all of recorded human history there are only about 37 years of peace, a pretty sad commentary on human nature. Think what this could mean if you could use it in the Middle-East, Northern Ireland, or even the American urban cities?"

"I know, I know, 'All we are saying is give peace a chance', blah, blah, blah. It's just that everything I've read, everything I've seen points to this book as a source of great riches."

"Some would consider peace to be great riches," Sam admonished, "and some already have enough of other riches." The slight jab was unmistakable, but Sam was too tired to engage in their usual subtle verbal tactics. "But, you know, if it's monetary riches you're looking for this capability has enabled the people here to become a central trade location. I imagine people flocked here from far away to take advantage of their negotiating abilities. That led to the unreasonable prosperity you see even today. It might be true that many fortunes are made in war, but many more are made in avoiding it."

She then left Chad alone in his solace and headed off to that wonderful tub that had been so good to her when she first arrived (not to mention several times since). This time she remembered to lock the door and conspicuously avoided touching the buttons on the wall. What she wanted most of all now was a little quiet time to digest all that had been happening.

A first it had seemed so ideal - Chad, this place, this work. In fact anyone looking into her life would say she was crazy not to snap it up as fast as she could. It seemed this offered her everything she could ever dream of. But that missing piece kept nagging at her. Sometimes, like when her life was heading in directions she didn't want to go, it was a blessing to have that feeling. It kept her focused on what she wanted, and gave her a sense of direction and purpose. Other times, like now, it was a curse. It prevented her from accepting what many would consider a pretty good life.

Leaving the library, however, had spoiled Sam from ever settling for "pretty good". She was after that rare life; the life lived joyously every moment. There was no way she could ever be happy with anything less now. Although this time with Chad had been, well, magical, she knew it was time to move on. He would probably be grateful to have the opportunity to get rid of her gracefully anyway, since now she would be associated with the greatest disappointment of his life. She earnestly hoped he would come to view the real secret of the book as more valuable than anything else he could have found, but that was for him to sort out for himself.

Sighing to herself Sam sank deeper into the tub and wistfully said, under her breath, "I will miss the sex though. He seemed to know everything I wanted even before I told him." There was a moment of mental hesitation as she briefly toyed with the idea of keeping him around as her "boy toy" but quickly dismissed it both as unfair to him and limiting to her. If she wanted to pursue her dream she couldn't be tied to something she knew wasn't right. The siren song of creature comfort would be a pull too hard to resist eventually, and she refused to allow that in her life.

She didn't see Chad at all that night. She figured he was probably sulking over his lost dream. It was

Rose in Bloom

understandable even though she didn't agree with his reasons.

In the morning James greeted her with breakfast in bed and guiltily informed her that Chad had departed the previous evening, having made arrangements for her return later that day.

It wasn't surprising to Sam that this news provoked no reaction from her. She had made her peace with her relationship with Chad and now she supposed that he had done the same, in his own way. She chose not to think of it as being dumped by the wayside, another in a long string of notches on his bedpost. Rather she knew that she was beyond this type of relationship and the fact that it ended so abruptly was simply proof of it. It would provide some fond memories for her in the future, but for now she would squeeze every last ounce of enjoyment out of the day before she had to leave.

Alone Again

After Chad left there was a strange hollow ring through much of Sam's life. It wasn't that she had lost anything important with him, but more that she had become more intensely aware of something she was previously oblivious to. Her own growth as a woman and as a person had given her that feeling often, but now she felt like she was on the verge of finally coming to a resolution – of settling into something that she wanted instead of avoiding things she didn't want. The search was on, and she didn't even know what she was searching for. She was absolutely certain of one thing though – when she found it, she would recognize it, and everything would change. Little did she know she'd find what she was looking for under the most unlikely of circumstances.

The coming days and months found her more and more occupied by her work. It was almost as if she expected to find her answer there, buried in the writing of people long dead. In truth it probably was there, but never obvious – always written between the lines and hidden in the things that were **not** said.

Rose in Bloom

The curator had only briefly talked about the incident with Chad. It seems that although he was most disappointed in the outcome of his search Chad was quite happy with being able to find what he had been looking for, and had moved on to other pursuits. No doubt he was still looking for those elusive riches. From snippets of conversation with the curator on the topic of Chad she had come to realize that he had been quite generous in praise of Sam and her work, and quite discreet about their private affairs. That was a pleasant surprise to her. Then she reminded herself that in his mind he was the one to dump her in the middle of Greece with not so much as a "goodbye" so his generosity may have been from guilt.

Whatever his reasons though, their relationship seemed to have ended civilly on both ends. He even smiled to her from across the room on the few occasions he had returned to the museum. She saw him now and then, off and on with a new woman on his arm, but never once did she feel any regret, nor any desire to rekindle what they had had so briefly.

The time passed, as it tends to do, and Sam's life rolled forward. She continued to date of course, but for pure physical pleasure it was hard to touch the experience she had had with Chad. The elusive connection she had been searching for seemed more distant than ever. Eventually she reached a point where she felt no particular desire to be with a man at all.

Hi Journal, it's been a long time since we've talked. I'm sorry I haven't been around more but my life has been so busy and so fulfilling that I didn't have the time. Funny, isn't it, how sometimes our lives get so full that we forget to live? Well I've been feeling a little out of sorts lately so I hope you'll forgive me for coming back to you just to vent a little.

All of the relationships in my life have led me everywhere I thought I wanted to be. Yet each time I arrived it was only to find out that, like chasing the end of the rainbow, the destination was only an illusion after all.

I think you know what I mean when I say there's a real hole in my life right now, and I'm starting to think that it will always be there. I've been with every kind of man you can think of, from shallow and dull, to thoughtful, provocative, and exciting. But none of them seem to be able to fill this hole. Am I being unreasonable, wanting too much from a relationship? Should I just settle for what I can get instead of searching for that elusive magical something, which may not even exist?

I know, I know, I'm certainly not about to find anything at all by refusing to continue to look. And you're right, the only real failure is the failure to keep trying. It's times like this I wish you could talk, to give me advice on what I should do next. Even if I didn't like what you had to say at least I'd get a different viewpoint and maybe be able to break myself out of this dungeon I seemed to have placed myself in.

Is there a key to get out of here? Is there something I have to do, or say, or learn that will free me? Maybe if I just open myself up more to new experiences. That was how I was after I left the library. I felt like the world was mine and I wanted to do everything I could that I had never done. Well now that I've done a whole lot surely there must still be loads of new experiences that I haven't found yet.

That's a good idea, Journal. I'll just drop the attitude of trying to find something that may or may not exist and just give myself permission to try different things for their own sake. Lord knows I was with enough men early on for exactly that reason – and none of your smart remarks, you know what I mean.

As usual you've been an inspiration. From now on I'm not searching for anything, I'm just going to experience what I can and enjoy it for what it is, not what I want it to be. Thanks again Journal!

Naked Strangers

Sam looked around at the naked bodies surrounding her. It was a surreal landscape of flesh and silk, almost dreamlike. This is the price of curiosity, Sam thought to herself. She never imagined this would be the result of a seemingly innocent action. None of them knew each other before arriving this afternoon and here they found themselves baring all to each other. The sequence of events that led her into this situation was a little hard to believe, even though it had just happened to her.

It had started innocently enough when Sam answered an ad in the local newspaper. It read,

> *WANTED: 20 intelligent unattached people for scientific experiment on human sexuality. We'll pay you $100 per hour for 3 hours of your time.*

Ordinarily Sam wouldn't have had any interest in such an offer, but something about it intrigued her. Sam's love life needed a little boost after Chad and she was feeling a little adventurous. Why, she wondered, would they want to specify intelligent people? I can understand

Rose in Bloom

the unattached part but how smart do you have to be to participate in a sexuality experiment? The promise of $300 was an added bonus. Sam daydreamed about using it to treat herself to something outrageous.

Sam copied down the number from the ad and put it into her purse. Doing so gave her a little "out" if she changed her mind later since it wasn't uncommon for her to leave things buried in her purse for weeks. That little trick had saved her from doing some dumb things in the past, but somehow she knew she would end up following through on this one. In fact she showed less restraint than she expected from herself, calling only minutes later from her cell phone.

After arriving home Sam set to making dinner. As usual she had forgotten to defrost anything so it was time to root around in the cupboards again. After several minutes of fruitless searching the phone rang. "Is it them?" she thought, with a moment of panic. "Hello?" she ventured, cautiously. "Good evening, may I speak with Mr. or Mrs. Sinclair?" "Sorry, nobody here by that name," Sam said gruffly as she slammed down the phone. Those darned telemarketers always called at the worst time.

Finally she found a large can of her favorite vegetable soup and some crackers that had not yet gone past their expiration date. The small pots clank noisily as she finds one to simmer the soup in and she almost missed the phone ringing once more. Checking the call display this time Sam verifies that this isn't someone trying to sell her long distance service or so-called "free" weekends at a time-share.

"Hello," she answers in a bit of a sing-song tone, suddenly a little bit giddy for no reason, while continuing to stir the soup. "Hello, this is the Rovivrus Research Foundation calling. We're calling for a Mrs. Sam Sinclair about an experiment she has shown interest in. May I speak to her please?"

"Well aren't they the polite ones," thought Sam. "This is **Ms.** Sam Sinclair speaking," she replied, being sure to subtly emphasize the "Ms." part. "Ahhh, my apologies Ms. Sinclair. I'm calling to confirm a time for your participation in our experiment. You are still interested are you not?"

The fact that he had caught her little correction and was even apologetic about it surprised Sam. Clearly this person was no mere phone drone. The fact that he was giving her the choice to back out confirmed that he was no salesman either. Sam's sharp intuition picked up on all this and judged that this organization was legitimate after all.

"I sure am interested, when should I come in?" Sam replied. The voice on the other end seemed to ease slightly from its former formality. "Actually this is rather short notice, and I apologize for that, but I assure you that it's an intentional part of the experiment. We'd like you to come in tomorrow at noon if that's possible."

Sam thought for a moment, instantly realizing that she was indeed free at that time but wondering if she was inadvertently about to step into a high-pressure sales trap. But no, her intuition had never failed her before and she was convinced this was a valid method of conducting an experiment, having been exposed to quite a few back in her University days.

"Yes I can be there. What's the address?" Sam wrote down the address and some brief directions on how to get there, then after exchanging a few pleasantries the voice on the phone excused himself saying that he had many more calls to make to complete the arrangements. Sam hung up slowly, a little bit excited now that the time was so near.

Looking down, Sam sees that her soup has been bubbling for a while. She quickly removes it from the stove and pours it out into her oversized soup bowl, pulls a nice big spoon from the drawer and sits down to dig in.

As she finishes her supper Sam starts to wonder again if she really wants to go through with it. The money would sure be welcome, but there were so many bad things that could fall under the heading of "human sexuality experiment". Sam was no prude – not by a long shot, which also meant she had heard plenty of things over the years that she would want no part of.

There was only one thing to do in a situation like this. Put a nice relaxing movie on and let her subconscious mull it over while she watched. Sam had a wide variety of movies she kept just for such an occasion. It seemed like something sensual was most suited to this particular decision so she selected the old standby "Bridges of Madison County" and fired up some microwave popcorn.

By the end of the movie Sam was much more relaxed and, as she always was after watching this particular movie, a little bit turned on. Thinking it through one last time she realized that the upside was a good chunk of money plus an interesting experience that might be fun. The downside was that she wouldn't like it and she figured she could either bail out early if it was really bad, or just suffer through it anyway and still get the money.

It was late at night when the movie had ended and Sam stayed up a little while longer in bed wondering what the experiment would involve. (Actually "fantasizing" would probably be a better word for it, and Sam's active imagination had no shortage of scenarios.) She finally drifted off to sleep dreaming of a handful of men with cute butts pampering her with a hot oil massage and oral sex that would make her scream with pleasure.

Sam woke up slowly, stretching like a cat and still smiling from the rather erotic dreams she had just had. She wondered briefly if when she returned she would need to make a booty call to a rather reliable and cute friend, or failing that treat herself to a warm stay with the shower massage.

Dreamily looking around the room her eyes fixed on the clock – then bulged wide as she saw that the time now read 11:30. She leapt out of bed, mentally calculating her driving time to be 10 minutes, which gave her 20 minutes to shower, change, and get out the door. "Well," she thought. "At least I won't be tempted to spoil the experimental results by spending too much time in the shower."

It was a bit of a rush but Sam knew just how to cut corners and speed things up to get out the door on time. Not her preferred way of doing things but occasionally a necessity. Hopping into her car she mentally pictured the route she would take and then took off.

Fortunately traffic was light, it being a Saturday afternoon and all, so she arrived pretty much on the dot of 12. There was a pleasant young girl waiting at the door to greet her, who then led her into a small room and gave her a sheet of paper to fill out.

The first section of the form was routine. Sam recognized it immediately as a gathering of background information so that they could classify the results by age, sex, and a few other things she thought odd but had no problem in revealing. Plus of course the usual disclaimer that she was here of her own free will and submitted to having these results published, yadda yadda yadda. Sam signed it and moved on to the second section.

This section was a little bit different. The questions weren't about her at all. They seemed to be more of an intelligence test. Sam thought to herself, "I guess this is how they're going to verify that we're actually intelligent and not just saying so." She knew full well how about 90% of the people would say they are above average in pretty much any area, including intelligence. Nobody ever wanted to think of themselves as "average" or especially "below average", even though just by definition of the word half of them would be.

Ironically enough this is exactly what you would expect when asking people about their intelligence. The more intelligent people would realize it about themselves, and the less intelligent people would not recognize real intelligence and hence also believe themselves to be above average.

Sam chuckled to herself as she ripped through the test. It wasn't easy by any means but Sam had qualified for Mensa several times in her past so a little test like this wasn't very intimidating.

Almost to the second when she put her pen down the girl who met her at the front door entered the room. She glanced briefly over the paper, trying not to be too obvious about looking through the test part. She looked up at Sam and smiled. "Looks like you've passed our first criteria. If you'll follow me please we'll just need to do a quick check on your health before the experiment begins. I'd also like to reassure you that if at any point you're uncomfortable with the experiment you are free to leave, but of course the $300 is only distributed at the completion."

Sam nodded, and was led into what looked like a doctor's examination room. After a brief wait an older man wearing a white lab coat entered, introducing himself as "Dr. Johnson". Sam couldn't help but snicker at the thought of a human sexuality researcher with that name, but quickly regained her composure.

The doctor explained that there would be a quick blood test and then they would apply sensors to Sam that would be required for the experiment. She responded by offering her arm for the blood test, but apparently all that was needed was a small prick of her finger. "Of course," she thought. "If they're going to complete the test before the experiment it can't be anything too complicated."

While the doctor peered at her blood sample through a microscope his assistant swabbed two spots clean on the back of Sam's neck and stuck on two small white circles that had some sort of metallic device embedded in them.

The doctor soon looked up from his study. "Those sensors that you now have on," he explained, "Have a tiny wireless transmitter inside them so that we can monitor

Rose in Bloom

your response without interfering with your, um, activity. You've passed the blood test with flying colours so the only thing left to do is to verify that the sensors work as intended. Would you smile for me please?"

Sam was puzzled at his request, but nonetheless was able to open her mouth into a broad grin. The readout behind the doctor blipped upwards slightly as she did so. "Excellent, now if you would, frown please." Thinking she understood how this worked now Sam put on her deepest darkest scowl and indeed the readout blipped downwards slightly. She tried to grit her teeth and snarl to see if she could make the blip move even further downwards. She could indeed, but only slightly.

Sam smiled once more and watched in satisfaction as the blip rose back upwards. Then she broke out into laughter and it climbed even higher. As she played this little game she noticed that there was a bright red line drawn across the display at a reading of '10'. "What's that line for?" ventured Sam, not really expecting an answer. "Put quite simply Ms. Sinclair, the experiment is over when you cross that line."

Before she could press for further information the doctor left the room. The assistant then instructed Sam to strip down and put on the robe that lay folded neatly on the table. Sam cautiously undressed then picked up the robe. It was hardly what one would expect in a medical environment – obviously silk and far more sultry than is standard.

"Maybe this is part of the experiment," Sam thought. "To see what I'll do with this." Alas no explanation was forthcoming and once she had donned the robe the assistant motioned her through a door that led into a hallway. She was instructed to go down the hall and enter the room at the end to await the start of the experiment.

Game On!

Tiptoeing gingerly down the hall Sam turned the knob and walked through the door. It opened up into a large room that looked like it would be more at home in a bordello than a medical facility. Big puffy pillows lay strewn all over the room. There was a fireplace on one wall, already lit and giving off a nice warm glow. The sweet smell of jasmine was in the air – Sam absently noted the incense burners sitting atop each end of the mantelpiece.

The lighting in the room was rather dim. Looking up Sam discovered why. On three walls of the room there was a narrow continuous shelf encircling the room and on that shelf were over a hundred small tea candles. The atmosphere in the room was oddly arousing – not at all what she had expected.

After completing her survey of the room Sam's focus switched and she noticed that there were women sitting in various places around the room. Most were scattered among the pillows. A few leaned against the wall or in the corner, apparently trying not to be noticed. All were dressed in a robe similar to Sam's.

One of the women nearest to Sam spoke. "Honey, you might as well make yourself comfortable. They told us to wait here for instructions and that this 'experiment' thing wouldn't be starting until all 10 participants arrived, and you're only number 7.

Sam graciously agreed and found a comfortable pillow to prop herself up on. She started to chat with the women around her, trying to find out what she could about what was going to happen. Each of them was apparently as much in the dark as she was. The only thing she could tell from the women themselves was that they had little if anything in common, other than the fact that they had all answered the ad looking for volunteers. "Prostitutes," Sam jokingly corrected herself with. As they were being paid they couldn't really be thought of as volunteers, and since it was a sexuality experiment of some kind that seemed the title that best fit.

Over the next 20 minutes or so the remaining three women drift in, one at a time. They too have no idea what this is all about and settle in to wait for the start. Sam notices that a few of the women lounging about on the pillows seem unconcerned with their state of undress, almost to the point of flaunting themselves. She of course was perfectly comfortable with her body, imperfect though it might be, but some of the women standing in the corner seemed a bit nervous.

Wondering if this tension might delay the start of the experiment, which Sam was now eager to get on with, she walked up to the wall and began chatting with the women there. Once she had confirmed with them that

Rose in Bloom

nobody knew what was going on she was able to talk freely, and it wasn't long before the whole room was alive with chatter like a women's locker room at the "Y".

Abruptly a voice boomed over their chatter. Apparently there was a loudspeaker hiding somewhere among the Persian décor. "Ladies," it intoned. "Thank you for your patience. I'm sure you're all wondering what this is all about, but before I explain what will happen I want to go over three important points that you have not been told as of yet."

There was a brief buzzing as everyone speculated to their neighbor what it might be and how outrageous it was that they had waited until now to spring these important points. "The first, and probably of most interest to you," the voice continued, "is that at the end of the experiment there will be one person remaining, and that person will claim a $25,000 bonus."

At this first revelation more buzzing erupted, even louder than before. Suddenly this experiment had become a lot more interesting but why, Sam wondered, would they need to do something like this when clearly everyone was already here just on the basis of the $300 promise alone.

"Secondly, and this will seem strange for now but bear with me, I must ask you all to remove your robes and place them in the container on the far wall." Even louder comments could now be heard but the voice went on. "We will understand if you do not wish to proceed further at this point, but it is a necessary part of the experiment. If anyone wishes to leave they may. You will still receive your stipend but your chance at the $25,000 will be lost."

A few of the women doffed their robes immediately and casually tossed them into the bin. Sam smiled at the nervous looking women she had been chatting with earlier and let her own robe slip off, sauntering over to the bin and gracefully dropping it in. They seemed hesitant at first but watching Sam's cool confidence seemed to spur them to action and they followed suit. After standing for a second together in the nude Sam could almost visibly sense the tension melt away. There was something about being in the company of other nude people that made your own self-consciousness fade.

After a short pause the voice returned. "Finally, and most important," it said, "the group will be larger than it appears." As soon as that last word faded out the far wall began sliding aside, opening up to reveal another, similar room that had adjoined theirs.

Squinting to see inside as it opened Sam soon realized that the other room contained a group of men that had been similarly prepared. They too were nude. Their room had beanbag chairs all over the floor, the same candle lighting the women had, and on the wall were famous portraits of nude women. Clearly they had been listening to an almost identical speech and were equally surprised at the wall sliding open.

Several of the women and a few of the men dove for cover. They propped up pillows to hide themselves, or stood in unobtrusive locations in an attempt to blend in with the décor. Sam was more curious than embarrassed, for looking around the room at the men she noticed the same lack of affinity among them as with the women. They were all different ages, sizes, and shapes. Had it not been for the fact that they were nude this group of men and women could have just met at a bar somewhere.

Sam found the situation a bit humorous, especially the people trying to hide, and couldn't suppress a giggle. Well if laughter is normally contagious the nervousness everyone in the room was feeling turned it into a downright epidemic. Within seconds the entire room was doubled over with laughter and even those that were attempting to hide had emerged, realizing that everyone here was just an ordinary person like them.

After a few minutes the laughter dies down and the voice returns. "We're glad you're all becoming more comfortable, and we'd like to offer this one last chance to anyone that wants to leave to go now before the experiment proceeds. There will be sexual contact involved and you need not participate if you do not wish to."

At this point everyone was rather relaxed, with the occasional titter arising as someone had an amusing thought. As a result nobody even made a motion to leave. In fact many of them had started to eye each other, no doubt wondering whom they would be able to get to "know" a lot better.

"Nobody wishes to leave? Excellent, then we may begin. No doubt you've all seen or heard of the 'Survivor' reality series, in which a group of participants are involved in various competitions, eliminating one at a time until a final survivor remains. That is what we're going to do, with of course the final survivor claiming the $25,000."

A muted muttering went around the room that seemed to have been anticipated by the voice. "Now I suppose you're wondering how we do this elimination, and what kind of research we are doing. Well of course you'll all realize that telling you the point of this would taint the results so you'll have to trust us on that point. As far as the elimination is concerned, that's where the sensors we've placed on you come in."

"These sensors," the voice explained, "measure the pleasure response. We have carefully calibrated each of them to reach the maximum setting at the moment of sexual orgasm. So in a manner of speaking you will 'vote yourselves off' when this peak is reached. The last one to reach orgasm will be awarded the bonus. As soon as you reach that point the sensor will beep and you must stop what you doing **immediately** and exit by the door in the center of the room. I'll emphasize this point, as failure to exit immediately will result in forfeiture of your $300 stipend as this is a crucial point in the experiment."

The room was abuzz with the muttering and mumbling of pretty much everyone present as they tried to wrap their head around what they had just been told. A million questions came to mind; of course all unanswered but there was lots of speculation to be sure. Sam listened to the chatter around her but was mentally puzzling over strategies to best win this "game". One thing she couldn't resist was a good challenge and this was one she would only get one shot at.

"Ladies and gentlemen," the voice broke in with, "I'm sorry for the subterfuge in bringing you all in. It was purely necessary to avoid the 'Survivor Syndrome' of having people self-select solely on their ability to make it to the end with no other redeeming qualities. We have carefully ensured each of you are intelligent, articulate, and in good health. Other than that you are a random sampling of the population; another factor vital to our experiment."

As the muttering dies down a few people make a motion to leave, heading towards the robe bin, but stop short after what appears to be a brief internal struggle. They've planned this experiment well. The carrot had been expertly dangled in front of them and now it was just too tempting to walk out on, no matter what they'd be doing to get it. Three hours after all was not such a long time, and it might not even last that long.

Sam glanced around the room once more with new eyes. She cunningly assessed the men and women who stood exposed before her. She knew she would have to fight her instincts to go towards the most attractive men in the room, that tall blonde guy in the back for example with the strong chin and tuft of hair on his chest. No, the first rule would be to gravitate towards those who didn't turn her on too much so that she would be able to last longer.

Sam snapped out of her reverie as the voice came on one last time to explain the rules. She listened intently, as did everyone else in the room, making sure to catch every nuance. It seemed relatively straightforward though. Any method of pleasuring is fair game. You could not leave the room for any reason or you would forfeit. When the sensor started beeping that was game over, no matter whether you felt you had reached orgasm or not. There was no appeal. You had to exit from the door in the center of the room and your clothes would be waiting in a change room on the other side.

The voice completed its explanation then informed them that the experiment had now begun and there would be no further communication to them. It was then replaced by some soft jazz music, no doubt carefully chosen for the purposes of the experiment. Sam imagined the researchers sitting in the back twiddling their dials and recording their data while this roomful of naked strangers tried to decide what to do with each other.

...

So this was how Sam found herself in this situation. The strangeness of it all was overwhelmed by the desire to claim that bonus. Everyone was looking around the room, milling about, trying to flesh out a strategy and looking for likely candidates. Sam had her own defensive plan set already, and it seemed like the most obvious offensive plan was to explore and find other people's "hotspots" and zero in on them. But how to do that when you knew nothing about the person you were with?

A petite blonde who had been lounging on the pillows made the first move. She walked boldly up to a shorter man standing on the other side of the room and whispered something in his ear. His eyes widened and he nodded, then the two of them went off into a corner and disappeared among the pillows.

Thinking furiously, Sam decided that her best bet was a younger man, probably just barely 20, who was sitting in the corner and sported an obvious erection. Reasoning that the younger men will have less control over themselves she guesses that a good rule of thumb is to stick with the younger ones. She walks quickly over to him, wanting to get there before the other women figure out what she's up to, and sits down beside him. She runs her fingertips over his feet, up his shin, behind his kneecaps, up his thigh and grasps him firmly in her hands.

By the look in his face Sam knows her guess was right. He's obviously turned on by this slight gesture and Sam gets an idea. She sits upright, positioning her lips next to his ear and whispers, "We both know you won't last very long in this game. Why don't you get some real enjoyment out of it at least and let me go down on you?"

The momentary pulse Sam feels in her fingertips tells her his answer even before he decides. After a moment's hesitation he realizes she is right and nods his head in agreement. Sam wastes no time, taking his earlobe into her mouth and sucking gently on it before running her tongue down his neck.

He tastes sweet, this young man, and Sam banishes the thought from her head immediately. "C'mon Sam," she thinks to herself. "Keep your head in the game, not in the clouds." Although she's never tried to apply her focus in this manner it's served her well in everything else she's done and soon she finds her head cleared of those thoughts. Meanwhile her tongue has wended its way down his almost-hairless chest to his navel and her prize is in range.

Sliding her hand down and out of the way she circles her tongue around his head. Spiraling down the shaft she makes sure his entire length is wet, giving her hands a nice smooth motion. One hand cups underneath him as the other strokes him steadily. Her mouth takes as much of him as she can in, since she knows this really drives the guys wild.

Sure enough it seems only a minute or so has passed when she feels him tightening up and his breathing increases. Her hand squeezes a little bit tighter and she hears him moan loudly as her mouth feels the warm flood of him letting go. His moans are interrupted by a loud beeping noise, which startles Sam momentarily. Quickly regaining her composure she sits up and lets go of him. "Sorry tiger, but you know the rules. I have to stop immediately, and you have to go. Thanks for the taste though, it was nice."

The young man looked a little disappointed that it was over for him. Sam knew he was probably thinking how he could have gone a couple of more times before he was **really** done but that wasn't the way the rules were written. He turns and exits out the door, being the first one to leave the room. Sam mentally congratulates herself and rests for a second to wait for her next "victim".

Looking around the room she sees all of the others have paired off by this point. One other woman appears to have tried the same ploy as Sam but she was not having as much success. The blonde that started first was on top of her man in the corner, going at a furious pace. Sam watched, almost hypnotized by the bouncing of her breasts and she idly wondered if they were real or not.

Within minutes Sam hears beeping noises from all directions and five more people, 3 men and 2 women, grudgingly get up and head out the door. Peering into the spots the 2 women emerged from Sam spies a man lying down, obviously abandoned just as he was getting into it. Slithering across the floor towards him she tries the same ploy, running her tongue up his leg, tickling his balls and then taking him into her mouth, tasting the sweet juice of the woman he had just finished satisfying.

Rose in Bloom

"Oh no you don't," he exclaimed, taking Sam's head in his hands and pulling her up to him. "We're going to do this on an even footing or not at all." Sam briefly resisted but realized she still had the advantage on him and locked her lips to his as she felt him plunging inside her. She had to admit that it felt really good, especially after her previous experience had left her wanting this all the more.

But back to business - Sam's focus changed and instead of enjoying how good it felt to have this man filling her she concentrated on squeezing and thrusting her pubic muscles. It was hard work, holding herself back and still trying to give him all the pleasure she could. She watched his eyes carefully for signs of sensitive motions, even as their tongues danced together.

Occasionally Sam would also look up and over at the other couples in the room. One poor guy had two women working him over; she knew he wouldn't be long. Another one had his head between a woman's legs as she moaned loudly alternating between "Oh No" and "Oh Yes", no doubt realizing that the intense pleasure she was feeling was balanced out by the fact that she would soon be out of contention, and sure enough when she stopped to breathe Sam could hear the beeping of her sensor that her moaning had been drowning out.

She continued to explore her current lover, looking for his pleasure points and little clues that he was weakening. His hands were the giveaway in the end. He was massaging her ass while she rode him, squeezing and kneading Sam but on one particular move she made his hands tightened on her. At this point Sam knew she had him. She alternated the move he was enjoying so much with a few others that she was able to do without too much stimulation to herself. Sure enough it wasn't long until his hands squeezed her so tightly she thought he would leave marks on her as he came hard to the tune of that now-familiar beeping noise at the back of his neck. Tempting fate just a little Sam gave him a few more quick squeezes, which he obviously enjoyed very much, before she stood up and left him.

As she freshened up her eyes again strayed around the room. A man with steely blue eyes met her gaze from across the floor. He was stunningly attractive. Sam examined him a little closer and saw that although his features were not that of your textbook "hottie" there was something about him that caught her attention. "Careful Sam," she thought to herself. "That kind of thinking is going to get you sent to the showers."

Fortunately for Sam the opportunity was not given to her as the feel of a warm pair of lips on her nipples startled her attention back to her own situation. She knew he was going to try to get his tongue between her legs in an effort to get her out without endangering himself, but Sam had an inspiration.

The blonde she had spied earlier was sending yet another happy but miserable man out the door when Sam caught her attention. She waved her over to join her. By this time she was indeed enjoying the warm attention of a hot pair of lips running around her pubic area. This guy knew what he was doing too. Her lips were on fire as he drew them into his mouth and his tongue penetrated deep inside, and then flitted about the surface in a teasing dance.

Knowing he would think he had won, Sam lowered him down to the floor, kneeling above him so that she was sitting right over his lips and they could continue their play. He didn't even notice the blonde arrive, or that Sam was whispering in her ear in a conspiratorial tone. She learned her name was Terry, and judging by the tone of her reply she was more than eager to try anything to win this competition. Terry smiled wickedly and nodded, circling around to the other side where Sam's benefactor lay exposed.

Sam couldn't resist turning around to look at the "horrible" fate about to befall this man of the talented tongue. Terry wasted no time, engulfing him completely in her mouth, making him hard in no time. She then almost pounced onto him, pulling herself up to her full height and slamming down on him again repeatedly. He was obviously shocked by this development and didn't know what to do, but as Sam had suspected in the end he just went with the flow.

Watching Terry's flexible and ferocious style on him made Sam briefly wonder if she had a chance against someone like this, but no – no sense giving up without a fight. The tongue and lips that had previously been driving so hard between Sam's legs had petered out to an occasional lick, no doubt just to help him hang on, as he was helpless under the onslaught from Terry.

Having her attention freed in this way Sam was again able to look around the room to see what the few remaining people were doing. The energy level had visibly declined since the start of this experiment as the effort of pleasing two or three partners had worn everyone down.

Once more Sam's eyes locked onto the man she had seen earlier. She was fascinated by the attention he was giving to his current partner, a fit looking brunette of about 30. The two of them were locked together and at first glance appeared to be enjoying each other equally. But as Sam looked deeper and paid more attention to the details she could see that he was clearly delivering the lion's share of the pleasure. His touch was soft, his kiss always elicited a shiver from her, and his hips always seemed to pause slightly before hers eagerly pushed hard against him. Once more a plot was forming in Sam's mind.

She barely heard the man under her cum, her own pussy muffling his voice as it was, but there was no doubt about where that beeping was coming from. Sam stood up quickly before he could regain his wits and moved to the side. "Thanks," she said to Terry. "I owe you one."

Looking right back into her eyes Terry said, "Well maybe I should collect right now!" Sam had expected something like this. A woman who was so intensely passionate in her lovemaking would surely not be hesitant to proposition another woman. This fit perfectly with her plan, fortunately.

"I don't know," she said coyly. "I've never been with another woman." That was only a half-lie – Sam was not counting petting and mutual masturbation, which she had done on several occasions and enjoyed every time. Terry was buying every bit of it. She stepped up to Sam and wrapped her arms around her, pressing her lips to Sam's as their breasts molded together.

"Wow," Sam said as she broke off from the kiss. "Y'know there are only two guys left and I bet we could make short work of them just like we did to this one." Terry giggled at the thought, but with a mock complaint said, "Oh but I'd rather enjoy what's between your legs than what's between theirs." With that comment she slipped a finger inside Sam and began twirling it in slow circles.

"Oops," thought Sam. "I'm losing control of the situation here, better go to plan B." "Is it really that good? I mean I've never tasted a woman before but I thought it wouldn't be as nice as having your lips wrapped around a nice hot shaft."

"Honey you just haven't lived until you've been between another woman's legs. She then reached between her own legs and rubbed a long slender finger around, dipping briefly inside until it was gleaming with her juice. She then reached up and traced the outline of Sam's lips with her finger and popped it inside her mouth. Sam eagerly sucked on it then said, "Mmmm… oh wow, you're right, that does taste good. But I don't know about the texture – it seems kind of weird when I take my lips between my own fingers. I can't imagine I'd like them in my mouth."

Sam had clearly hooked her on the thought of introducing Sam to the pleasure of knowing a woman. She wordlessly put her hands on Sam's shoulders and pressed down until Sam was kneeling in front of her. Then she lay back on the pillows behind them and drew Sam's head into her. Smiling to herself Sam extended a tentative tongue onto this woman's neatly trimmed (and not blonde!) pubic hair, tracing the edges of her soft skin.

"Don't be afraid," Terry said from above her. "Just dive right in – you'll love it." Meanwhile one of the two remaining men was approaching them, obviously liking what he saw. "Silly boy," thought Sam. "This is the last place you want to be right now."

Taking her cue and being careful not to appear too eager Sam's tongue slipped further inwards. She felt the smooth texture of the short hair against her tongue, then followed the outline of her lips the way she had traced her pubic hair earlier. The taste was familiar from Sam's earlier experiences but the feel of her tongue against it was something new - something very nice too. She ventured a quick motion, running her tongue from the very bottom of the opening right up past where her clit was through to the top of her pubic hair. It elicited a satisfied sigh from Terry who, still in the role of the teach said, "That's it, that's the spot. Nice isn't it? Keep doing that."

Sam looked up and saw the man that had approached them, Chris she remembered his name was – at least that's what the redhead he had been with earlier had been screaming out. Chris had his mouth wrapped firmly around Terry's left nipple. She seemed to pause for a moment, assessing her own situation, then deciding that even with Sam between her legs learning all about the pleasures of a woman, and this guy who obviously knew what to do with her breast judging by the tingling sensation he was arousing, she was in no immediate threat so she sat back and enjoyed for a minute.

Taking the opportunity to do a little exploring, Sam carefully mapped out the "terrain", making a mental note of each little spot that made Terry twitch but not staying too long at each. She wanted to give the impression

Rose in Bloom

that she was nothing more than a pleasant but harmless distraction.

It appeared to be working as Terry's attention shifted more to Chris. Her hands were reaching down his chest, stroking his bare skin and eliciting goosebumps as she went. Sam was a little aroused watching her do this – she was obviously very talented at making people feel good. She knew what would happen next and wondered idly how she would be able to do it.

It wasn't long before she got her answer. Moving quickly and decisively Terry wrapped her arm around Chris's leg and shifted him sideways. His weight was pulled out from under him and Chris was helpless to resist. In one smooth motion Terry pulled him close and had swallowed him right up to the hilt. Sam's eyes popped out in amazement as she did that. Not only at how she was able to take the whole thing in her mouth but how fast she was able to do it.

Poor Chris didn't have a chance now. Sam could see by the look that came over him that he had lost all thoughts of winning and was lost in the enjoyment of Terry's tongue. He idly reached up to take her breast in his hand, but Sam could see it was more for his own pleasure than for Terry's.

Knowing this was her chance Sam quickly mapped out a plan of attack. Watching Terry's rhythmic motions she matched her own tongue pace to it. Sam knew that by doing this she would remain undetected until she moved in for the kill.

To his credit Chris lasted quite a long time inside Terry's talented mouth. Several minutes elapsed before Sam saw him start to tighten up as orgasm approached.

This was her chance. Sam dove in to Terry, matching her own earlier ferocity, hitting all of those spots that she knew would drive her wild. Terry seemed to hesitate for a second but the flood of Chris's cum into her mouth distracted her again – Sam knew from watching her earlier that Terry greatly enjoyed that sensation and would hang on to get every drop.

Meanwhile Sam continued her attack, her tongue darting swiftly between Terry's legs, sliding upwards and swirling around, then returning to her original spot. Over and over she did this until she felt Terry quaking beneath her. Her orgasm was obviously going to be as intense as those she gave to others. Her hips were bucking hard now, as Sam vaguely registered the fact the Chris had left after Terry was finished with him (and long after his beeper first signaled him to leave).

Sam hung on to Terry's soft rear, pulling her face tightly into her as Terry bounced and turned, almost screaming each time Sam completed her swirling motion. A faint beeping noise could be heard between her screams and Sam knew it was over. Terry however was not letting go, grabbing Sam's head and pushing her hips hard into her. Figuring she might as well finish what she started Sam kept up the same motion that had driven Terry to this point and soon felt a second, harder orgasm.

At this point Terry had been drained. She clearly wanted Sam to continue but no longer had the strength to insist. Sam sat up beside her and whispered in her ear "Thanks, you were a good teacher. I hope I got an A." Terry faintly smiled back at her and replied, "A+ and a capital O. It's hard to be disappointed with something like that, even if I didn't win this little contest. Maybe we'll run into each other on the outside." With that Terry stood up and walked a little shakily, but still with a visible wiggle, out the door.

And Then There Were Two

Looking around Sam confirmed what she feared would happen. The only two people that remained were she and the tall man with the steely blue eyes. She had been watching him carefully (well, as carefully as possible given what she had been doing) and knew that he had been doing the same to her. He was resting on the other side of the room, sizing her up this very minute.

Realizing that if he had seen her at certain moments he would know exactly what to do to ensure his own victory. Sam hoped he had been distracted at those times for she knew that although there were definitely things he preferred she never saw a serious enough reaction from him to call it a weakness.

Knowing she was at a disadvantage she decided to go on a cautious offensive. She slowly approached him from across the room, pretending to look at the candles (almost burned down now), the pillows (strewn randomly around the room), and the door that one of them would soon leave through.

Rose in Bloom

Thinking that keeping her distance at first would be a good ploy she offers her hand and introduces herself. "So, my worthy opponent. I'm Sam, but considering the situation you can call me Sam. Pleased to meet you," she said, mentally adding "And I'll meet you to please you." The inner pun made her smile and a bit of her worry vanished.

The tall man put out his own hand and replied, "Hello Sam, I'm Ken. I suppose you've been watching me as much as I've been watching you. I hope you also like what you see the way I do." His handshake was firm yet oddly soft. "He must have an office job," thought Sam. "Um, Sam... my hand?" Sam quickly let go, realizing that she had allowed herself to be momentarily distracted. "Uh-oh, not good," she thought as she blushed. "Time to change tactics."

She walked right up to Ken and, standing on her tiptoes to reach, whispered in his ear. "Yes I have been watching you, and I do like what I see. I've liked it since I first walked in the room. I look forward to giving you much pleasure."

"Sam, Sam, such an obvious ploy, feeding my ego. I had thought an intelligent woman like you would have figured that much out by now." Sam was somewhat taken aback by his response. "Double uh-oh," she thought again. "Am I really that transparent?" Being called out like this gave her a little respect for this man standing in front of her. He obviously didn't play games. This was someone she could deal with on her own level.

"Well Mr. Ken the mind-reader I guess you caught me. Since I won't be able to put one over on you I might as well be honest. I do indeed find you quite attractive, and under different circumstances I would even consider dating you. However we're here for one thing and after watching you with the other women I'm curious about what they found so irresistible about you."

"That's better Sam," Ken chuckled. "But you're wrong. We're not here for one thing. We're here for two things - the prize money obviously, and to provide as much pleasure for the other person as we can. Would you like to hear my theory on what this experiment is all about?"

Again Sam was surprised. She had forgotten all about the experiment, being caught up in a series of moments. She mentally chastised herself – knowing the purpose could have brought an easier way to get to the end. Still, Ken had been thinking about this so she was curious. "Theorize away Mr. Smarty-Pants."

Sam knew saying that was a mistake. It revealed a weakness, -that she had not been thinking about the purpose. Ken showed no sign of noticing however, and his demeanor remained as cool as always. "I believe we are here to see how the pleasure response is altered when one person sincerely wants to please the other. The money and game was just their way of providing the motivation for us to do exactly that. In a way we've been behaving in a selfless manner, but for selfish purposes."

Pondering this for a moment Sam realized that it made a lot of sense. That certainly had been her approach all along, even to the point of denying herself pleasure in order to bring more to her partners. That sparked a thought and Sam added, "I see what you mean. Then the little sensor has two purposes. It measures the information

Rose in Bloom

they want to collect, and serves to cull those in the group that got more than they gave, so to speak."

"Exactly," Ken agreed. "Not only that, but the fact that we were changing partners often and that we've all never met before meant that we couldn't use an attachment or reasoning as the basis of our behavior. It had to be all driven by basic instinct."

"So what do we do now that it's just the two of us?" Sam queried. "You mean now that the rats have figured out that they're in the maze?" Ken chuckled in response. "Well it's my turn to be honest. I've been attracted to you since I first saw you as well. I can't even explain it. No offense but several of the women were more physically attractive so that wasn't it. It was just something about you; the way you carried yourself with confidence maybe, or the gleam of intelligence that shone out of your eyes."

Sam didn't know how to take that. Surely he couldn't be trying to pick her up since the fact that they were about to have sex was foregone. He must really mean what he's saying. She has no answer for him and they both stand silent, gazing into each other's eyes. "Oh my god," thought Sam. "I can't be falling in love with him. Not here, not now."

She decided to test the waters a bit and brought her hand up to the side of his head. As she gently stroked his earlobes he mimicked her, bring his hand up to her head as well. Sam was afraid to do anything further, but wondered briefly how his chest would feel beneath her fingertips.

At that moment Ken reached down and ran his hands across Sam's own chest, fingertips dancing nimbly across her breasts, lightly tweaking her nipples. Sam flushed again. Could he read her mind as well? Automatically she responded in kind, and so it continued. Each move she made he would follow, and every place he touched on her she immediately touched on him. They were two kindred spirits exploring each other in a way that was both platonic and highly sensual at the same time. At least it was as platonic as possible given their current state of undress.

Sam felt a stirring deep inside her, but she didn't recognize it as sexual desire. This was something different; something primal. She was about to throw caution to the wind and put a voice to her feelings when Ken spoke. "I know what you're feeling, because I'm feeling it too. We seem to be connected at some level beyond normal perception. I don't know about you but I've learned to always trust this kind of feeling. The ones you can't explain are often the most powerful of all."

"Aren't we the mystical one," she managed, halfheartedly and not at all sure she was joking. Once again at a loss on how to proceed Sam furrowed her brow in frustration. Ken picked up on this immediately and echoed his own frustration at their situation. "So what do the rats do," he said in mock seriousness, "When they've discovered that there are more important things in the maze besides the cheese."

Sam ventured, "We could just quit the game and leave," silently adding, "and pick up in privacy somewhere." Ken replied, "Yes, we could. But if the sensation fades it may never return in exactly the same way. I've dedicated my life to choosing errors of commission over errors of omission. I'd rather make mistakes than lose important opportunities by doing nothing. I have an overwhelming

Rose in Bloom

desire to make love to you here, and now, and no really good reason not to."

Responding in the only way she can Sam stood in front of him and slowly raised her lips towards his. Inching ever closer, slowly so that they had that last opportunity to stop and leave the game. But Ken had already been clear that he was not going to resist and his lips eagerly met hers. Sam's world exploded in a blaze of fireworks as they drew each other close and buried themselves in that kiss.

The moment seemed to stretch out to infinity. The two of them, lips tightly joined, tongues playfully dancing together, and their naked bodies pressed together. Sam could live in that moment. She suddenly wanted nothing more than to ensure this man with her was given everything she had to give. She wanted him to smile at her, to laugh with her, and she wanted to see the joyful look on his face as they made love.

The two lovers immersed themselves in their passion. They were barely aware of anything but each other as their intensity rose higher and higher. At one point Sam vaguely knew that he was giving her the same pleasure that she was giving him, but it didn't matter. The two of them were merging, anticipating each other's thoughts and desires. He knew just where she wanted to be touched and she had him at her mercy. A voice in Sam's brain was screaming to her THIS IS IT, DON'T YOU RECOGNIZE IT, THIS IS IT but she was too lost in herself and Ken to figure out what the voice was trying to tell her.

Somewhere in that passion Sam noticed that both of their sensors had been beeping. But that was impossible

- she was nowhere near orgasm. She ignored it, figuring her heightened state had somehow fooled it. Ken showed similar indifference to anything outside the tiny world they both now lived in. The moment was everything and only they shared it.

It was Ken who realized what was about to happen. The room was empty, the sensors were signaling, the game was over. In minutes the researchers would be in to tell them the results and shoo them on their way. Reluctant to give up his world but realizing that it would soon be out of his hands he whispered "Solare" into Sam's ears. She nodded and repeated it, only dimly aware of what was happening.

Just at that moment the "exit" door opened and three researchers in lab coats came in. The familiar voice from before came over the loudspeaker and informed them in a cool collected voice that the experiment was now at an end and they would be required to leave.

The lead researcher was less cool as he frantically shouted out, "WHAT DID YOU DO?!??!" Sam was returning slowly to full awareness so Ken asked the obvious question, "Do with what?" "With the sensors of course. You must have been fooling around with them. They blew the top right off of our scale!"

Ken decided to play dumb, answering, "I have no idea. We didn't touch anything so far as I know. Maybe your equipment is faulty. But since you're here you can tell us who won. We were a little … ummm … distracted." He mentally snickered since he knew full well what had happened to their equipment. He and Sam had connected on a level their sensors were not designed to register, in effect overloading their "pleasure scale".

Sam is now listening intently to what is going on and quickly pieces together the details, coming to exactly the same conclusion as Ken. She follows his lead, asking, "Yes, who did win? One of us gets the final prize money now, right?"

The voice returned over the speaker with their answer. "Ms. Sinclair, you were the final survivor by a margin of only fractions of a second. You may exit through the side door and get dressed to claim your prize." Ken jumps up, saying, "Ah-ah-ah. I was out before you so I get to leave first." He quickly sneaks out while the researchers in the room examine both of their sensors for possible malfunctions, talking animatedly among themselves.

This day seemed to have lasted years considering all that had happened to her, so Sam was grateful when she was finally able to leave. To her disappointment Ken was already gone when she stepped into the change room. She quickly donned her clothes and went out to the entrance where a smiling young lady awaited with her cheque.

Sam couldn't resist asking, "So now that the experiment is over – what exactly were we being tested for?" The lady smiled and responded; "I guess it's okay to tell you now. We were performing a psychological experiment in human sexuality to determine if the pleasure levels were on average higher when a person is more considered with pleasuring their partner than themselves. And I must say with the exception of the final two of you it indeed showed that in spades. We're still trying to figure out what you did in there, but it certainly wasn't expected."

Smiling to herself Sam mentally patted herself on the back for figuring out what was going on in there, even if she did have a little help. As she walked down the street though she felt emptiness. It was easy to explain of course. The connection she had felt with Ken was so deep and so intense that it would remain with her always. If only he hadn't left so quickly.

Pacing slowly ahead Sam realized she was famished. No surprise there given how much energy she had probably burned off. She watched the restaurants go by along the street. McDonalds, Starbucks, Solare, The Mandarin, ... Wait a minute - that last name looked familiar. The recollection of Ken whispering it into her ear came flooding back. Dare she hope?

She fairly flew back to the restaurant and gingerly opened the doors. Sure enough, waiting at the hostess station was Ken, breaking out into a broad grin at the sight of her. She leapt forward and embraced him in a big hug, squeezing him as tight as she could. Looking up into those hypnotic eyes again she said, in a voice calmer than she felt, "So, are you going to buy me dinner while we discuss what to do with *our* money?"

Ken was obviously not surprised at the implication that they would be sharing the prize as he smiled back down at her. "Later my love," he answered. "For now let's just figure out how we're going to tell the tale of how we met to our children, and our grandchildren." Linking arms they strolled off to the table to talk of the future.

Printed in the United States
130583LV00001B/3/P